Chase sits at the round table in Dr. Puretzky's intro to Film class. Dr. P is scribbling on the board, and chalk motes hang in the sun rays.

Parker walks in with Nikki.

Chase looks at her with a wry face. *Of course she'd show up in the one class I might enjoy.* In her white coat and fur hat, she returns the same expression.

During class Nikki and Parker write comments on the edges of their pages for each other. The way they avoid looking at Chase confirms what they're writing. And Parker has, in fact, decided she'll pass this semester by punishing Chase. Granted, he came to Canada last summer, after their falling out. But she believes it was guilt motivating him north. Last semester, he could have made things up to her in a million ways, and he tried not one.

When the bell finally rings, Chase shrugs on his coat, puts on sunglasses, and slides past Parker and Nikki.

"Hello," Nikki says sweetly.

He puts a hand up, smiles sarcastically, and moves around them. When he looks back, Parker is shaking her head at Nikki, who's shaking her head back. *Girls.*

But he fears Parker is no longer just "angry." It's possible she hates him. *Oh, it's going to be a long semester.* If he didn't love film, he'd switch. Although even if he did switch, he needs her to stop hating him. Parker's violet perfume follows him down the hall like a bad dream.

DON'T MISS A SEMESTER ...

THE UPPER CLASS

MISS EDUCATED

OFF CAMPUS

CRASH TEST

CRASH TEST

AN UPPER CLASS NOVEL

HOBSON BROWN, TAYLOR MATERNE & CAROLINE SAYS

HARPER TEEN

An Imprint of HarperCollins*Publishers*

The authors would like to thank their agent, Sally Wofford-Girand, and their editor, Zareen Jaffery. Caroline Says would also like to thank The Edward F. Albee Foundation, Ledig House, The Constance Saltonstall Foundation for the Arts, and The Ucross Foundation.

HarperTeen is an imprint of
HarperCollins Publishers.

Crash Test

Library of Congress catalog card number: 2008921074
ISBN 978-0-06-085085-2

Typography by Jennifer Heuer
❖
First Edition

*This book is dedicated to the freaks and geeks, stars and
losers, the heirs and heiresses, the scholarship students and
the postgrads, the mathletes, the hipsters, the theater rats,
the art snobs, the future I-bankers and the future criminals
and the future philanthropists and the future celebrities, the
dictator's daughters and the senator's sons, the supernerds and
acidheads, the trustafarians, the* Mayflower *descendants, the
Prep for Prep kids, the ones who tripped and fell, the ones who
got up, the ones who hit the ground running, the ones who ran
out of steam or hope or luck or cash, the ones who treated the
others like dirt and the ones who loved everyone around, the
ones who got lost and the ones who got found, and every other
soul who has ever passed through boarding school gates.*

1

New Year's Day. Room 414. Miami. Pizza box on the black marble bathroom sink counter, e-z wider rolling papers on the floor. The orange dust of Adderalls crushed and snorted off the white bedside table. The stink of toxic boys sleeping late.

"*Shit*, let's hit it, guys," Chase says, bloodshot eyes taking in the huge wet stain in the closet where he pissed by accident last night, sleepwalking and drunk. "Um, we need to jet before someone sees this."

Greg, Gabriel, and Chase stagger with luggage into the elevator, where a woman in Burberry shorts murmurs to her rhinestone-collared Chihuahua. In the lobby Greg sinks into a white leather club chair, knees spread wide, talking—as usual—to Delia on his cell.

Gabriel and Chase lean against the counter, desperate to check out. They keep looking behind them.

"Should we really head to the camp? I don't know if Noah wants us to come," Gabriel says.

"Oh, please," drawls Chase. "Why wouldn't he?"

Gabriel has on his serious face. "I'm just saying."

The clerk gives back Gabriel's Black AmEx. "Thank you, Mr. Velez. *Do* come again."

"We're going," Chase says to Gabriel. "He's our *boy.*"

"Okay, okay."

They half run through the hot parking lot. Once they get into the car, they can breathe. They know they're in the clear. Gabriel tears out. Chase lies in the back of the 6-Series BMW convertible, its mica charcoal paint sizzling in the sun of the open road. The sky is reflected in faux aviators he bought at a gas station.

Chase is happy to be with his boys, after all the girl drama last semester. He looks at the pair. Gabriel, in tortoiseshell glasses and a Lacoste shirt, a Rolex Daytona on his thick, hairy wrist. Driving this fast car and blasting Rihanna. If Gabriel was only a dilettante from Colombia and not a too-serious-son-of-a-public-figure-who-gets-death-threats kid, everyone might be jealous. As it is, Gabriel is growing up too fast and stepping into big political shoes too soon.

Greg is priceless. With nubby hair grown out from the shave of football season to protect his dome from New England winter, girlish lashes, coffee-bean pupils, and a temper. He's not as fit as he was at the season's end, because he's been eating candy bars like they were going to stop making them. But he's still massive, still muscle. Around his neck hangs a gold chain and a charm in the shape of Cat Island in the West Indies, his mom's hometown. Greg's white wifebeater is bleached against his black skin.

"Home free, suckers!" Chase calls out to the roaring wind, and Greg yodels back.

The exhaust of I-95 further clogs Chase's sinuses. Some girl with pink hair and pearls made him do lines on a balcony last night; *Happy New Year, baby*. He didn't know her name. They looked at the skyline and cracked jokes about turning into pumpkins as the sun rose, and he lost her, or she lost him, and it didn't matter. It was that kind of party. Nameless and beautiful.

A week's worth of images click: The Setai, Gabe's cousin Dominique with scarlet lips, raw sea urchin at Nobu, Lil Jon at the pool, Jessica Alba escorted from a black Tahoe SUV into a private villa. This trio is dead set on starting the year with a bang. So far, so good.

"Hey, douche bag." Greg turns to Chase. "You got a smoke?"

Chase puts his hands on Gabe's shoulders. "That, my friend, was a sick time."

Greg laughs. "Sure was."

Chase pulls out his Parliaments. "Dominique. She's got by far the prettiest Catholic ass south of the border."

"You better watch it, kid, that's family," Gabriel says, eyeing Chase in the rearview.

They whip past the Palm Beach exit, where Wellington students congregate over Christmas break to sip Belvedere Greyhounds in Lilly Pulitzer and banana-yellow slacks. To the Wellington crowd, the Breakers might as well be Bethlehem. Chase smiles slyly: *The Red Cross Ball? Please, we had a suite in Miami across from four Brazilian models. I pissed at a urinal next to Nas. I watched Fergie get into a helicopter.*

When he arrived at Wellington a year and a half ago, he was blown away. His brother, Reed, had been a prep-school star, helping to convince Chase that life is all about Brooks Brothers and hedge funds. But somehow Chase grew disenchanted with silver spoons. So far, his boarding school stint has only been trouble. Every day he becomes more of an outsider. He's not meant to be so straight and narrow, to live so buttoned up. *Give me some raw life, some new territory.*

And Chase fell in awe with the streets of Miami. Drag queens strutting past Dumpsters. Cuban guys playing dominos. Black girls in satin and lace, their gold platforms shining in the streetlights, cell phones strapped to their ankles like guns. He stared at the glittering, derelict crowd pushing up to the McDonald's counter around five A.M. The women leisurely looked Greg and Gabriel up and down, and play-fully scoffed at pale, lanky Chase. Which only made him want them more.

Chase spent the previous lonely semester holed up in his room, gloomily reading about free will. He'd decided that what had been missing from his life, what might have kept him out of so much trouble, was a guiding principle of his own. So he checked out library books by Sartre and Hobbes. Studied Hindu philosophy. And Hunter S. Thompson.

Now, Chase is all about carpe diem. He's devoted to pursuing what he believes, and what he believes happens to be that he has a right to pursue what he believes.

This is heaven, in between the road and the sky, in between one Florida town and the next. Chase's hair is honey-streaked and too long, as it was before the symbolic crew cut last spring, so he shakes it out of his eyes. He's a Prep-School Cowboy. His work is done in Miami. On to Rexford Collegiate Lacrosse Camp, in Cocoa Beach.

Cocoa Beach. Hiltons and Doubletree Hotels interspersed with motels with dirty neon signs advertising vacancies. A Ron Jon Surf Shop sits next to a Midas garage. Stray dogs piss on palm tree trunks.

"Interesting," Greg says. "We may have to bring this place to life a bit ourselves."

Porters attack Gabriel's car, and the guys check out the pool. Chase fixates on a mother and baby.

Greg is unimpressed. "I hope we didn't leave Miami for family vacation."

Chase grins wickedly. "I am *not* done yet. I need to close out this trip with some fucking dynamite."

"Well," Greg says, smiling, "I have a feeling we can turn this place out."

They rent surfboards from the hotel shop. The sand is soft and grainy. The waves light and clean. Chase floats. Surfing reminds him of Mal Pais, of Parker, skinny-dipping in moonlight, body shimmering like a mermaid. Her kisses made more impact than sex.

He rides one in. Gabriel and Greg clap on the shore. He waves, triumphant, as he lets the board sink in the shallows, and he falls over with pleasure. Last semester really *was* a lonely blur, with Gabe, Noah, and Greg in Eliot, and Chase exiled in Summer. Gabriel got tangled with Nikki; Greg fell for Delia. Noah made new friends.

As Chase finally paddles in, Gabriel and Greg are chatting up girls in bikinis. And Chase smiles; he's back with his boys. *Don't let go of this.* Deep in these thoughts, Chase doesn't see the shadow. It has to be eight feet.

* * *

"Jesus Christ. How did you not see that thing coming?" Greg asks later, still laughing, as Chase ices his temple.

"I don't have eyes in the back of my head." Chase sneers, and glances in the mirror. The scar looks like a *Z*. He feels tough.

"Not too bad, right?" Chase points at the cut.

Greg barely looks. "I've cut myself worse shaving."

Defeated. He gives Greg the finger.

"So Gabe chatted up these girls," Greg says, looking out the window now, his black hoodie, stitched with white skulls, open to bare chest. "I guess their whole team is at the camp. I told them to roll by the beach at nine."

Chase pours from a vodka jug, his board shorts dry and salt-starched. "Cute?" He mixes lemonade into his drink.

Greg grins. "Cute for you. Not for me because I'm *married*."

Noah has no idea that delinquent visitors have descended on his turf.

Rexford is where top prep schools and private schools send their lacrosse teams for early training every winter. The facilities are manicured, packed with athletes. On one field, Noah makes an assist to a postgraduate, or "PG," an athlete who graduated elsewhere but attends boarding school for an additional year to get into a better college. O'Mara is a stocky redhead; he's UVA bound, and a Wellington celebrity. Like most PGs. They *should* be famous; they've experienced "normal" high school. Made out with girls in cars. Pulled bongs in basements. Sat down for spaghetti dinners with their families. Crazy stuff.

Chase, Gabriel, and Greg watch the game, lined up, in sunglasses, smoking.

"Noah's killin' it out there," Greg says as he bites into a Taco Bell burrito.

Chase nods. "He's doing good. He shall be rewarded."

Noah catches sight of them; he waves, grinning at those freaks of his and also feeling his heart sink at the prospect of trouble. The exhibition ends with little fanfare. Wellington outscores St. Christopher's, a private school from Richmond, ten to one.

Noah jogs over, black hair kept out of his face with a green bandanna. "Yo. You actually came."

"Of course, dude," Chase says. "We gotta do some celebrating since you missed New Year's. *Which*, by the way, was nuts."

Noah nods. "I can only imagine. What's the plan tonight?"

Greg grins. "I loaded up Gabe's room with booze, so I figured we'd just meet on the beach in front of our hotel."

O'Mara slaps Noah on the ass. "Nice goals, dude." He looks at Gabriel, Greg, and Chase. "Gents. What brings you down here?"

Chase smiles. "Just visiting our boy. Might have a little thing on the beach later, so come by."

O'Mara smiles back. "Cool. I'm in."

As the big athlete lumbers to the showers, Noah turns to Chase. "Chase, dude. Don't tell *everyone*. I'll get booted if I get caught, and some of the guys on the team don't party."

"Jesus, Noah. Calm down. I told O'Mara. One person. And he definitely parties."

Noah gives in when Chase steals his stick and gloves and starts faking plays and crowd applause. And truthfully, he's just relieved to have the old Chase back. Last semester, Chase moped around campus with a chip the size of an asteroid on his shoulder. Noah tried cheering him up with weekend binges at his family's NYC apartment, but Chase was such a moody SOB that he even managed to piss off Noah's old St. David's friends. Noah hoped that Chase's black cloud would lift, and it has. He isn't the kind of guy who would give up his first friend at Wellington. Noah has learned to take the good with the bad with Chase, because the good is often worth the wait.

Last year the two spent countless nights lounging in one or the other's room having midnight conversations about topics like Boy Scouts, soldiers, cell mates. Talking about vintage Mustangs, girls with bangs, nitrous hits. They've traded rugby shirts, shared meatball grinders and Maine root beers, passed a copy of *Jarhead* between them.

Each one is starstruck by the other's world. Chase likes to hear New York City stories about rich kids sniffing heroin, about autumn days spent in Central Park watching swans and smoking joints, about models, penthouses, a shoot-out in Chinatown, a car crash on Park Avenue. Noah's met Tom Ford and Gisele and Karl Lagerfeld, as his dad works in the luxury business. He's wandered through art studios and grimy bohemian walk-ups, while his mom buys art. He watched, from the grand window of his uptown apartment, as the towers burned.

Chase tells tales of duck hunting on Southern rivers, of mint juleps served in silver cups on plantation porches, or horses being shot after breaking a leg, of working dogs and true belles of the ball and the ghosts of slaves drifting down twilit dirt roads. Chase can be overbearing, for sure. Noah is often the only one at a table still listening to one of his longer diatribes about Kant or Kerouac or Abbie Hoffman. And Chase taps him for money all the time. *Pay me back one day, dipshit,* Noah says with a smile.

But once in a while, during those late-night sessions, Chase was more honest with Noah than he had ever been with anyone else. He admitted defeats. He spoke about how he and his dad didn't get along. Or the day his brother poured gasoline into Chase's fish tank. Once, when Chase was thirteen, he was at a friend's house and stumbled upon his friend's mother in the laundry room. The morning sun made her negligee glow, and she let one strap slip as she folded a towel slowly. Looking at him. No one had ever looked at him like that, except from the pages of a magazine. And he backed away, watching her face turn derisive, and he ran. He flew out the front door, kicking over a stone urn, spilling the pink-petaled geranium inside.

Chase is hungry for destruction and hedonism. The trio start drinking in the room as sunset paints the walls. Each has the devil in his eye. Hours slip by. They walk down to the beach, where Noah is sitting in the sand with a crew of players—guys and girls.

"What's up, boys?" Noah grins, raising his hand.

The city's electricity creates a lavender horizon against the night. iPod speakers hum over voices on the dark sand. The girls are from Richmond, and their accents are sugary. One of them tells Chase she doesn't like the music.

He scoffs. "It's Interpol, come on. Just because you're Southern doesn't mean you can't listen to angry, ironic bands from the Northeast."

Gabriel passes out beers from a cooler, cheekbones lit by the hotel's light, his Von Dutch trucker hat turned backward. O'Mara arrives with a group of guys in tow.

"O'Mara!" Chase shouts, sensing a fellow troublemaker in the PG.

O'Mara grins. "Where the fuck you been? We've been

sitting on the patio, eating ice cream, for Christ's sake."

"We're right here, my friend. You thirsty?"

Ah, and the games begin.

A little deeper into the night, Chase is slurring, explaining his surfing accident. O'Mara, another PG named MacArthur, and a few guys are left, as well as two girls from Maryland. Greg and Gabriel are practically rolling in the sand, drunk and crazy. The majority of athletes realized there was beer and liquor, caught a whiff of marijuana on the coastal breeze, and slunk away. Chase was sickened by their cowardice.

"I thought it was twelve feet, but when it closed in, it looked bigger. I just couldn't get out in front of it." He sips his beer and sighs. "Sucks too. Woulda been a sick ride."

O'Mara raises his glass. "To the twelve-footer Dobbs let slip away."

Noah stands apart, his white pants phosphorescent in the night. His body aches. He's exhausted. He's annoyed he didn't make it clearer that it wasn't the best idea to show up here with drugs and booze and bad intentions. At a *sports* camp.

Noah watched some players climb the dune earlier and shake their heads when they saw him with a beer and a cigarette. This is one week, *one week*, of hard-core athletics. What's the point of being here if not to perform? A few guys stuck around, but only the PGs are getting as stupid as Noah's friends. The brunette puts her hand on Chase's thigh.

Noah tosses his beer can and starts down the hill. He knows that Chase gets belligerent and demanding the later it gets, and Noah always kept up in the past. But he's beat. He's out.

He passes Greg and Gabriel, stripped to boxers, lighting sticks in the bonfire and running around with them like drunken Indian chiefs.

"We're hitting the ocean, Noah," Greg calls out. "Come with, yo."

"Uh, can't do. I'm kicked," Noah says.

And he ends up in his room, lights off, listening to his roommate snore. Hearing music and laughter. He's missing the party, but he's safe from stupidity.

And stupidity is what comes next. If it weren't for Mac-Arthur, everything might have been fine. *Maybe.* It's hard to tell, and after the story circulates through the prep-school system, there's less clarity than at the beginning.

The basics are this: Around two A.M., MacArthur tries to take a girl to the room, which is against the rules of the camp. He's a 6'4" lacrosse star from a Massachusetts public school, with a Celtic tattoo on his inner calf. She's a tall blonde in a tie-dye tunic. They're not an inconspicuous couple. In the lobby, she starts singing and tripping, and the concierge calls Coach Butler.

After MacArthur leaves the beach with his blonde, Chase and O'Mara laugh in the hot tub as the remaining girls unbutton wet shirts. Chase rolls his eyes when O'Mara asks the girls to kiss like on a spring break MTV show. But he watches.

Chase is on his way back from pissing in the dunes, rounding the building to jump into the tub, when he hears voices. Butler pulls O'Mara from the steamy water. O'Mara laughs like he doesn't care. He'll care tomorrow. He even grabs at his beer. MacArthur stands, chagrined, beside Butler, having been hauled out here from the lobby. The girls cover up with towels.

Chase trips down the beach, unseen, stoned on fear, unable to look back.

The bathtub is his coffin when Chase wakes up to Greg peeing next to him, morning light streaming through the blinds.

Greg looks down. "Heard you come in. What a night, am I right?"

Chase tries to laugh.

"How'd you turn out?" Greg asks.

Chase shrugs. "You want the long or the short?"

Greg zips. "Hopefully the long, right?"

"Not exactly." And Chase tells the story.

When Chase tells him about Butler pulling O'Mara out of the hot tub, Greg is shocked. "They didn't catch your ass?"

Chase shakes his head.

"You think they're going to tell?"

Chase shrugs. "They can't even prove I was there. Honestly, I don't think the guys gave a shit."

"They might give a shit now."

Greg and Chase pack in silence. They down Advil and Emergen-C. A three-beat knock is Gabriel. When Chase swings open the door, Gabriel swaggers in, lights a cigarette, and sits down.

"What's wrong with you, Dobbs? Did you not get your own Southern belle?"

Greg shakes his head, and Gabriel knows something's wrong.

"Oh, shit. What happened?"

After Chase tells the story, he feels a little better. Gabe and Greg don't see any enormous problem. It wasn't really his fault. He was just lucky to have been gone when the thing went down.

Noah gets word of O'Mara's and MacArthur's demise at morning practice. The coach reported the rule-breaking to the school, and neither PG will be returning to Wellington. And they certainly won't be scoring goals all semester for the team. By lunch Noah's getting stares and mumblings.

Was this his fault? He hadn't even been there then.

As they load the bus for the afternoon game, Noah sees Gabriel's car about to leave the parking lot, and he jumps down the metal stairs.

"Yo. You all taking off?" Noah asks, leaning in the window.

Gabriel nods, lifting his tortoiseshell glasses. "Catch you back at school, my friend."

"You hear about O'Mara and MacArthur last night?" Noah asks.

Greg laughs. "Heard about it? This asshole barely escaped." He points at Chase.

Chase grins sheepishly. "What can you do, right? Kid wanted to get laid and he got caught."

Noah stares at the ground. Of course it was Chase who ruined the season. King of the fuck-ups. *Love you, man, but you sure know how to make a mess. I knew something like this would happen.*

"Guess you're starting now; no more bench-sitting for you. You can thank me later." Chase lies down in the backseat, shirtless, his Madras shorts filthy and leaking sand from the pockets. He shields his face from the sun with a magazine. He wonders if Noah is pissed.

"Yeah, I'll do that," Noah says, smiling wryly, waving them out of the lot.

The bus is silent when Noah steps on. He's stunned. No one looks at him. He takes a seat in the back.

"Be sure to thank your friends for ruining our fucking season." The voice is low and monotone.

Noah stares ahead as if he hadn't heard.

Noah feels like a wishbone, brittle and yielding at the same time. Pulled from one side by Chase, and from the other by the team. The guys on the bus can't be serious, though—no one makes another person drink, or smoke, or fuck up. And besides, off-season, these players party harder than anyone. They just get self-righteous when their own scorecard is at stake.

The bus trundles through tropical smog, and Noah is miserable. He's surrounded by crew cuts, jock itch, bruised shins—and guys hating on his best friend.

One night last fall, he and Chase walked out into the woods. Some freak student from another era—renowned for taking acid during his final exams—built a tree house in the school woods. Noah and Chase climbed up into it, steam puffing from their mouths, and felt like pirates in a crow's nest when they got up there. The gold-lit campus was land, and they were at sea.

They stared into the sky, comfortable enough to scour the heavens in silence. They looked for a design in the mysterious chaos, like millions of boys on millions of nights from a myriad of vantage points had before them.

"There it is," Chase said.

"Orion," Noah answered, discovering the constellation at the same moment.

2

Parker's semester doesn't open with a bang. It opens with a bit of blood.

Her bags aren't unpacked yet. She didn't have the heart to drag out the books and wool sweaters and vintage T-shirts and notebooks, and commit them to that room again.

Instead she stands in Happer Woods, picking tobacco from her lip as she smokes. Gray—that castle of girls—looms on the hill, its golden windows like eyes. Although in truth she can't be seen; one just *feels* watched on this campus.

She adjusts the fur hat over her ears. It's a lot of things out here—dark, wide, empty, starry—but it's not warm. On her floor, girls are probably making hot chocolate in their pajamas, gossiping. The house of sisters is giddy to be reunited.

Nikki and Delia seem resigned to be back. Nikki's still 100 percent Long Island, in oversize Gucci sunglasses and a Juicy Couture hoodie, her nails French manicured. She's healthier than when she arrived last year, toned and rosy from chopping and planting on Woods Crew. And wiser. Delia's gained a few pounds, from late-night pizza and vinegar potato chips, and is growing dreads. But she hasn't lost her California gold-dust shimmer.

Delia and Nikki love Parker, even if Parker exists slightly on the outside of the duo. Nikki always braids her long hair. They ask her to do I Ching and tarot, and watch, mesmerized, as Parker turns over cards with angels and executioners. They look through her records, which have thrift store stickers on their sleeves, and her books on owls and Brazilian street gangs and herbal medicines. They try on her pomegranate lipstick and elbow-length black satin gloves. It's the Parker Museum, full of oddities and treasures.

And Parker respects Nikki and Delia. They both faced monsters here. Schuyler wrote hate mail on Nikki's skin. Delia's dirty past—real and rumored—trailed her here like toilet paper on her shoe's heel. The girls kicked their demons. They're survivors.

Delia and Nikki each have the North Star of being in love. Nikki has Seth, even if he's in New York, and Delia has Greg. Parker has a guiding light, too: Chase. But she navigates by hating him.

"Shit." She smokes in the dark.

While home for Christmas, she said *shit* one too many times. Her mom pulled her by her velvet sleeve into the kitchen on New Year's Eve. Parker had been kicking the coffee table while her baby brother, Finn, drew snowflakes in his sketchbook. She'd had a few beers earlier with Pete, her ex-boyfriend-but-still-friend, in his beat-up truck as they looked over the plains of Ottawa. She'd had enough Labatts to make her surly as the buzz faded later.

It's not the language so much as the negative attitude, her mom, Genevieve, had said. *What's gotten into you, Park?*

And Parker tried for a hopeful shrug, but it fell flat.

You act like you feel sorry for yourself, Genevieve continued.

Finally, Parker looked her mother in the eye: *Man, I just don't want to go back there.*

And that started a discussion that lasted an hour.

Why not? Baby, what's the issue?

Parker hated how much it cost the family. She hated being far away. And *some* of the students believed they were born to inherit Park Avenue and the Pentagon and the palace of the American dream. Parker loathed entitlement. *No,* she thought when rich kids strutted down marble halls. *You got lucky. That's how you ended up here. Now you have to make good on it.*

Even some kids who work hard annoy her. They're robots, competing for four-point-ohs. Parker's parents are brilliant hippies. Her house is full of books and records and maps. Dinner conversations revolve around fauvist art and Japanese punk rock and shooting stars and snow leopards. She likes to learn and read and think and debate. But she's not an automaton, battling for commendation by the Wellington throne.

And then there's the problem of Chase. *Ugh.* Everything she loved—the devil-may-care snarl, the pretty-boy face, the doe eyes that go dark when he's bored or jealous, the swagger of a younger brother forever bullied, the slouch that says: *I'll stay here or go where I want, thank you very much*—these things are now reversed, like a negative photograph. All that love now equals hatred.

At last, she'd teared up. *Mom, I don't belong there.*

And her mother had relented. *Oh, sweetie, you can come back, you know. You don't have to stay.*

By then it was Parker's turn to say that she should finish the year. She didn't want to run back to Canada with her tail between her legs. When Parker arrived two Septembers ago, in tiger-print pants and horn-rim glasses, she didn't think she'd last the day. That first week, at yet another welcome-to-Wellington-you-should-be-grateful-we-let-your-ass-in-here assembly, she'd been shaking. Nikki took her hand, and Parker cried. No one had touched her since her dad kissed her good-bye. And she was used to lying against Finn on the couch, their cat, Raisin, warming both of them, their parents cooking in the kitchen, an old record spinning in the other room.

These black woods are still, and wetness creeps up her blue jeans. Her paranoia is so extensive that she sees eyes in the bramble. Okay. Now she's really cold. And she's pushing Check In. She stomps the butt out and looks at the imaginary eyes.

They close.

She loses her breath.

She starts walking toward the vision, the body. And there's a whine. She gets close enough to see; it's a dog. Laid up against a fallen tree. She strikes her Zippo: blood on the snow. He bares his teeth.

She lets the flame go out. Her heart is pounding.

"Hey, there," she murmurs.

His gums shine as he growls.

"Hey, love. I'm not going to hurt you."

His eyes shut. He's too tired to fight, or he's giving up.

"Oh God," she frets. "Hang on."

Gingerly, she stoops over him. One eye opens—barely—and the lid drops. His lips hang. His teeth are pink with blood. Her hands are shaking from cold and fear, and she holds one to his nose to sniff. A mortal courtesy. He does not react.

And so she goes further, and wedges her fingers under him. He's not warm. His nose twitches and black lips quiver.

But he either doesn't have the heart to battle or he succumbs because this is his only chance.

He's a small, dense dog, like a cow hound. His ears are pointy like a pig's. She holds him to her chest like a sleeping five-year-old, struggling with his weight, and walks as briskly as possible on snowed-over roots. She emerges from the woods and hikes up the incline, breath like blue smoke, toward the gold lights. She's heaving by the time she gets to Gray.

"Hey!" she yells at the stone building.

At the front door, Parker waits. She can't put the dog down. Eventually she kicks the door with her boot's heel.

"Hey," she shouts again.

Katie Liesl comes to the door, toothbrush in hand. Her eyes widen.

"Get Mrs. Jenkins," Parker says.

When the housemaster arrives, Parker's arms are giving out. Mrs. Jenkins looks at the dog and the girl on this snowy night.

"Oh dear," Mrs. Jenkins says. "What happened, Park?"

"I found him in the woods. I think he's dying."

Mrs. Jenkins chews her lip, tucks red hair behind her ear. "Can you put him down?"

"I'm afraid to. Can we just take him somewhere? Do you know a vet?"

"All right, you know what? The Vasherney Animal

Hospital should have an all-night vet on."

"Please, can I come? I don't want to leave him."

Mrs. Jenkins hesitates. "Okay."

They put a fleece in the back of her Subaru, and Parker lays his body on it gently. He twitches.

They drive—snow pushed to the shoulder, farmhouses sliding by. Parker calls the hospital on Mrs. Jenkins's phone, gets a groggy woman. They pull into a lot, one light shining on the cinder-block building. A woman with a bun stands at the open door, her white sleeves shivering. She comes to them with an animal stretcher, leans it against the car.

"Is he yours?" she asks.

"No, I found him in the woods."

The vet touches the dog's throat. She doesn't say anything.

Mrs. Jenkins and Parker hold ends of the stretcher while the vet takes the dog in an embrace, and transfers him. Immediately the stretcher's white canvas starts to absorb a splotch of red. Now the vet holds the door and directs them to a room. In the clinical light, Parker looks at this animal—beautiful and ruined. His eyes ice-blue slits under black rims. His hide is speckled like tortoiseshell.

"Let's see what's going on," the vet says, feeling his body with gloved hands.

She gets a weak snarl as she tests his back leg.

Parker feels tears well up. "Is he going to be okay?"

The vet continues examining him. Then she looks at Parker. "I'm not sure. He's in shock."

"Did he get hit by a car?" Mrs. Jenkins asks, her brow furrowed.

The vet takes off her gloves and leans against the metal counter. "I think he was probably beaten, then thrown onto the highway or something like that. He's just a pup. Must have been too many in the litter. Happens all the time. If you look at his face and back, he's got scars. It looks like he's been through it."

Now Parker does cry, and Mrs. Jenkins pats her back, a bit awkwardly, as they barely know each other.

"I'm going to keep him overnight, obviously. Let me see what I can do." The vet speaks kindly but firmly, unwilling to make promises, unwilling to make excuses for the laws of nature.

Parker cries most of the way home. Mrs. Jenkins lets her. She keeps looking at Parker and then at the road. When Parker's sobs have lessened, Mrs. Jenkins smiles.

"Strange way to start the semester, isn't it?" Mrs. Jenkins says dryly.

Parker can't help but laugh. She wipes her eyes. Her sleeves are stained with blood. Yes, it is a strange beginning.

"And it wasn't safe, you know, what you did. Animals are frightened when they're hurt. It can be dangerous to save an animal in pain. And we'll let the reason you were *in* the woods slide." Mrs. Jenkins gives Parker a stern wink.

Parker sniffles, and smiles.

Parker feels a shyness, or a crush, with her housemaster. She wants this person to take care of her, but knows, of course, that Mrs. Jenkins is not her mother. She looks at the teacher's white hands on the steering wheel. The woman is squiring her, taking her to a semblance of home, at least. Parker thinks of her mom's hands too, how Genevieve remembers to take off her soapy rings halfway through washing dishes. The clack of a wedding ring when she picks up a phone. The wrinkles on her knuckles, grooves that have been cut into her daughter's heart.

3

econd week of school. Airplanes cross the frozen aquamarine sky. Students wear duck boots, the hoods of their jackets pulled over their faces.

Laine has somehow landed in the Girls Varsity Ice Hockey tryouts. She's here partly at the urging of her therapist, Anne, who wants her to try new things. Laine's been seeing Anne since she got back to Wellington after the 60 Thompson nightmare, and finally it looks like Laine's moving beyond the nosebleeds and compulsive running and midnight puking and the need to say the right things or nothing at all.

And Dr. Puretzky coaxed her here. *Your stick skills, your athletic ability, your sense of the game—you're going to be first line, Laine. You just have to learn how to skate.*

Ha! she thinks. *Just have to learn how to skate.* The ice gleams like an impossibility. From rafters, pennants sway. Everything echoes—especially Dr. P's whistle when he signals the girls to race to the sideboards. *Here we go.*

Laine's arms flail like chicken wings as she works across the rink. The other girls glide, arms swinging, touch the boards, and make sweeping turns. Laine crashes into the boards, then makes the clumsy journey back. She's heaving and red.

Dr. P blows his whistle for the other girls to take laps and he stands with Laine.

"Good job, Lainer."

She looks at him with sarcasm in her blue eyes. "Yeah, right."

"I'm serious," he assures her. "You gotta start somewhere. Now let me show you something."

"Okay," she says, lifting the front visor of her helmet.

He crouches on his skates. He smacks his thighs like meat. "The key to good skating is being grounded. Get down like this, in a chair-sitting position."

She bends her knees.

"But get your weight centered; you're leaning forward too far," he says, demonstrating. "You gotta *sit*."

She does it and he claps. "Yeah, that's it. If you stand tall, you get knocked down. You sit, you're close to the center of gravity; you can get bumped around but you're not going to topple. You're powerful."

Next he shows her how to push out of sitting, shoving each skate away by the inner blade.

"This is where your power is, as a skater. It's in the thighs."

He skates in slow motion, and then twirls to face her. "You go."

She sits deep, then pushes one skate left and the other right. And her body feels it, like a key clicking in a lock. *This is how you do it.* Just then, her blade catches a crevice, and she takes a digger, spins on the ice. Even getting up is a debasement, and she kneels like a child, pushing herself up with her stick, falling, and then standing.

From the bleachers, Noah and two other Varsity guys are watching. Noah's black North Face jacket is unzipped, his cheeks rosy. God, he used to think Laine was "pretty." Just "pretty." Now he can't take his eyes off her.

"That's the way!" Noah shouts, unable to keep quiet.

Oh, how dare he watch me, Laine thinks. She *is* learning not to obsess over perfection. But not when Noah Michonne is watching! It's not like she *likes him* likes him. But she doesn't need his long face and black wavy hair and deep eyes turned in her direction. This week isn't the first time, either, that she's felt his eyes on her. Whenever guys observe her, she can't help but feel like meat in a butcher case, trussed with string.

In the locker room, she steps into the shower. Lets water stream over her. Laine has stellar genes, *Mayflower* DNA. Her dad's dad married a Swede, injecting angelic, wintery beauty into the sometimes dumpy, hard-jawed WASP stock. Laine was magnificent from birth, with Mediterranean-blue eyes and white-blond hair. But she's not assured of this, and doesn't know how to use it. In her dark hours, it doesn't save her.

She's more diligent than smart. People *have* made blond jokes about her. When she's focused, her mouth hangs open. Her teachers say she'll catch flies. Her hands are so small a piano teacher said she couldn't perform pieces that require reach. Her voice is scratchy, like a smoker's. Meanwhile, one drag would make her feel dirty.

Laine looks best on a horse. In jodhpurs, a red jacket, and a black velvet helmet, she could be an eighteenth-century heroine. Her intelligence is in her legs, in her grasp of the reins, in the molecular-level movements she makes to communicate to the animal. She is physically brilliant. Born elegant—if not articulate.

She towels dry, barely registering her own body. It's amazing how many times a day she still tumbles into the belief that she's not good enough. That she'll never be good enough.

* * *

Out of her window Parker sees Mrs. Jenkins walking up the snowy path, steam twirling from a coffee thermos, red scarf around her neck. Parker greets the housemaster at the dorm's front door.

Mrs. Jenkins smiles. "Hey, there. So I talked to the vet. His back leg is cut deeply. She has it bandaged, and she knocked him out with pills because he was trying to get up. But he's okay. You saved him, Park."

Her face flushes. "I can't believe it. Can we go see him?"

Mrs. Jenkins looks at her watch. "I can't today. Tomorrow maybe."

"When can we bring him back?"

Mrs. Jenkins smiles ruefully. "Parker! This guy, he might be aggressive—he's been mistreated, you know? We have to think about getting him adopted by a good family. We need the shelter to test for aggressiveness. We need to pay his bill."

Parker's heart sinks. "You mean I can't keep him?"

"Are you kidding? You can't name one student in the history of boarding schools who had a pet."

"Dawn had an iguana last year."

"That's different."

"*You* don't want to take him?"

"I'm not really in the market for a dog."

Parker makes sad eyes.

"Listen, Park, I'm not saying anything now. We'll discuss this. Okay?"

"I'll take him for walks and work him out and feed him and everything if you keep him," she says really fast.

"We'll *discuss* it."

Parker can tell Mrs. Jenkins wants to get into her apartment. Her husband, Mr. Jenkins, is here; he comes on weekends, as he teaches at Yale. They're attentive to students but nothing more, and all weekend the kids smell lavish meals, exotic spices, and rich flavors coming out of their apartment, uncurling like love itself. He's balding and bespectacled, but they look good together. Smart and alive and happy for each other's company.

"I'm sorry," Parker says.

"Don't be *sorry*," Mrs. Jenkins says, as if confused by Parker's statement, and slips through her door.

Parker turns away, thwarted. She drags her feet to her room, flops on her bed. Nikki's writing at her desk, sweats rolled to her calves and hair in a ponytail on top of her head.

"What's up, babe?" Nikki says, without stopping her work.

"Ugh." Parker sighs. "I want what I cannot have."

"Oh, sweetie," Nikki says. "You and everyone else."

Parker laughs as only Nikki makes her laugh. Outside the window is a crisp night, and she's cozy here in their room. But the dog has become everything, an omen and a reality for Parker. If he comes back to her, Parker will make it through this hard winter. His face looms in her imagination: ugly and marked and true.

That first month of school is evil cold. New classes, new teachers, sussing out new crushes in new classrooms. Chase heads out of his dorm into the white world in Ray-Bans and a camel-hair coat, with his morning Red Bull. Sleep crystals are caked in the corners of his eyes.

He's taken heat for Florida. The first day back, Trevor Houston, senior captain of the Varsity lacrosse team, sent Chase (and cc'd the team) a "thank you" e-mail for "personally ruining our chance of a New England Championship." Trevor promised he and his teammates would pay him back. Chase hasn't talked with Noah about the threat—because he doesn't want to know more, and because Noah might still be pissed, and it's better not to bring it up.

Summer is the loser dorm, where Chase was placed to keep him from making trouble in fertile territories. Nerds are now returning from classes or spilling out of the building, with their graph paper pads and sci-fi fantasies and unpopped zits.

"What's up, bro?" asks Levi, in his enthusiastic Lower-form way.

"Calm down," Chase answers as they cross paths.

Chase's drawl has only increased, as though he's hanging on to a world of sweet tea and Cajun catfish and red sunsets and low country and shrimping boats. This January air can't freeze his heritage out of him.

Dr. Puretzky's Intro to Film has a long wait list but Chase got in; someone dropped out and he got a note in his box yesterday. Chase sits at the round table. Dr. P looks like Dustin Hoffman, and his New York accent is strong. His hands are bear paws. He's scribbling on the board, and chalk motes hang in the sun rays.

Parker walks in with Nikki.

Chase looks at her with a wry face: *Of course she'd show up in the one class I might enjoy.* In her white coat and fur hat, she returns the same expression.

"Okay, class. Let's not waste time."

Nikki and Parker write comments on the edges of their pages for each other. The way they avoid looking at Chase confirms what they're writing. And Parker has, in fact, decided she'll pass this semester not by knitting or playing sudoku but by punishing Chase. By raking her nails down his soul—her new hobby. Granted, he came to Canada last summer, after their falling out. But she believes it was guilt motivating him north. Last semester, he could have made things up to her in a million ways, and he tried not one.

"We've got fifteen masterpieces on our plate," Dr. P says.

He goes over the syllabus, naming Charlie Chaplin's *The Kid*, Kurosawa's *Ran*, and Scorsese's *Mean Streets*, among others. Chase tries to lose himself in this decadent list. When the bell finally rings, Chase shrugs on his coat, puts on sunglasses, and slides past Parker and Nikki.

"Hello, dumb-ass," Nikki says sweetly.

He puts a hand up, smiles sarcastically, and moves around them. When he looks back, Parker is shaking her head at Nikki, who's shaking her head back. *Girls.*

But he fears Parker is no longer just "angry." It's possible she hates him. *Oh, it's going to be a long semester.* If he didn't love film, he'd switch. Although even if he did switch, he needs her to stop hating him. It's partly ego; he's always won ex-girlfriends back as friends. He doesn't like a bunch of females bad-mouthing him; it's bad for business. Her violet perfume follows him down the hall like a bad dream.

That girl. Noah is more pleased with his draw of sticks. He's sitting across the table from Laine in economics, her hair tied back, cheekbones gold from Christmas vacation. She's one of those girls who doesn't mean to be beautiful. *She can't help it. It's annoying.*

From the overhead projector, percentages are displayed onto the screen, but nothing can compete with Miss Cashmere Turtleneck. Her blue eyes are electric in the darkened room. *She'd better stop nibbling the goddamn pen. How come everything she does makes me horny? She could smell her own feet at the dinner table and I'd ask for whatever she's having.* It still doesn't make sense to Noah. Last semester they were barely buddies. Now he can't stop thinking about her.

When the lights come on, Noah grabs his books, catches up to her. *Shit, now it's time to act.* They walk toward the clang of the dining hall, not quite together but not apart.

"Hey, good job on the ice the other day," Noah tries.

Laine halts. "Are you trying to further embarrass me?"

He holds up a hand in defense. "No, dude. Honest. It was cute."

Her cheeks turn pink, and she thrusts her chin forward. "Whatever."

"I'm serious!" Noah says.

"Yeah, I realize," she says.

He laughs, looks for a guy to commiserate with, but there's no one. He dallies at the coat hooks in the hall's entryway so she'll be ahead in line. Noah simmers with impatience. *This should not be so freakin' difficult.*

"Hey, man," Gabriel says, sidling up, his polo collar popped under the blazer.

"What's up, bro?" Noah says.

They stand with trays, shuffling to the steaming buffet, and chitchat—but Noah's thinking about other things. He wonders how Chase had the balls last year to just up and take Laine for himself. Noah is forever studying Chase. *Why have I always been a wingman? Why can't I step up like the others and get what I want?*

Noah was raised in Manhattan among über-wealthy kids. Maybe it's that Noah's dad is French, or that his parents are happily married, that has made the difference. Noah and his two sisters traveled the world, listening to adults talk at dinner tables without dumbing it down, walking through museums with their art-gallery-owner mother and actually looking at the paintings. Noah, Anais, and Colette were taught to be polite, curious, gregarious. While their friends clamored for Pop-Tarts, they tried goat yogurt, cactus apples, and sweetbreads. They're a stylish family; today Noah's wearing a Dries Van Noten jacket and Miu Miu loafers. They have a few good pieces each, and take meticulous care of them. The European way. They say "please" and "thank you." They actually mean it.

"Oh, boy," Gabriel says, of a somewhat European sensibility himself. "Another glorious meal of chicken fingers."

"Man, I might just have cereal; that stuff looks nasty."

Noah's reserved, yes, and jealous of his buddies back home who own the world. What Noah doesn't know yet is that those guys are one-trick ponies. Take Frederick. Even at four, Frederick ran his home. At dinner, his parents and their guests answered every nonsensical question of his as if he were an esteemed gentleman. His mother, who could make corporate executives cower, would not say no to Frederick. He's the king. If Noah looks closer, he'll see that all the kings he knows are turning into sociopaths. Noah should covet his own discipline, his manners, but that's a hard thing to do when you want someone as badly as he does.

As very, very badly as he does.

He looks at Laine as she inspects a plum. The shimmer of hair. The doll waist, pinched by a tweed skirt. The leather boots. Should he learn to be like other guys, and reach out and take—with force—exactly what he wants?

His parents' good friend Joy married a corporate pirate. He was atrocious. He started eating before everyone was seated. Picked corn from his teeth. He even once conspicuously raised a haunch to fart silently at the table. Everyone loved to make fun of him when he wasn't around, and Noah's parents condemned his business tactics. They had always coached Noah to wait his turn, to be honest and forthright, to leave the last piece of pie. But God knows, Mr. Corn Fart was living in a Fifth Avenue palace, and Joy was spoiled and content. Noah was once stuck in a cab with him, and the guy started handing out free advice. One morsel stuck in Noah's mind.

Here's the secret, the raider had said. *Most people don't know this about themselves. They* want *to be taken over. It's their deepest desire. You're doing them a favor.* Noah thought that was the most menacing thing he'd heard. And at the same time, he feels now like Laine *does* want him to pursue her. She just doesn't know it.

4

January unfurls, cardinal by cardinal, evergreen by ever-green. Kids eat soup in bowls with the green Wellington crest. They break in textbooks, write their names in high-lighter. Catnap in common rooms by the light of the soda machine. College applications pile up in colored folders, essentials written on the tab: DEADLINE, PRIORITY, DOCUMENTS NEEDED. This is business. The business of one's future. The business of prep school.

"Working on it," is what Mrs. Jenkins always singsongs before Parker can ask.

The dog is better, physically, but the school might not allow him in the dorm. Parker thinks of him, caged in a white room, afraid. On top of every other injury, he's alone. Parker watches Mrs. Jenkins get out of her Prius with a blue yoga mat, or salt the path so the girls don't slip. Parker presses her forehead to her cold windowpane on the third floor.

"You're obsessed," Nikki says without looking up from her algebra work.

On Sunday afternoon, Parker cross-country skis the wooded trail into town. It's a backward errand, doing athletics to buy tobacco, and she hocks up loogies. She unlatches the bindings when she reaches the village, carries the skis over one shoulder on the slushy sidewalk. The town isn't busy, although the stained windows of the church glimmer, and there's activity inside. New Englanders aren't shut down by snow. She watches now as an old Wagoneer with tire chains clanks slowly up Main Street, a white-haired man puffing on his pipe, letting the greenish smoke out the window as he drives. He represents the casually stoic townspeople.

At the gas station, she leans her skis against the glass storefront and walks in the door, the bell ringing in her bad intentions. Parker scans the room, empty but for a tall kid in a porkpie hat checking out the magazine rack. *No threat there.* For some reason, perhaps because she doesn't look typically Wellington, they don't card her here. A teenager with the slack belly of someone who's recently given birth looks dully at her, eyelids smeared with lavender.

As they begin to make their transaction, Parker hears the bell. She drops the pouch of Natural Spirits tobacco on the counter and steps back from the cashier, like a panicky animal. Parker can't believe her bad luck.

Mr. Grant is headed straight for her. Not just any teacher, but her favorite—the astronomy professor and Woods Crew leader.

"Hey, are you checking out or not?" the girl asks.

"Hmm?" Parker asks, and peruses the Tampax section.

"Hello, Miss Cole," Mr. Grant says in his New Zealand accent. "Those your skis out there?"

She smiles, heart hammering. "Yes, they are actually."

"Do you mind if I jump ahead? I'm in a hurry."

Parker nods her head. "I'm not in line. Still shopping." She holds up the Tampax box. *Awkward.*

"Oh, okay." Mr. Grant sounds confused.

Suddenly the guy from the magazine rack steps around Parker. "Go ahead, mate," he says nonchalantly to Mr. Grant. "That's mine, there. I was just picking up more necessities." He holds up a bag of Blow Pops and a six-pack of Genesee Cream Ale.

"Thanks, guy." Mr. Grant hands the attendant a twenty. "Diesel, for the Suburban. Parker, you need a ride back to school?" he asks on his way out the door.

"No, I'm fine, thanks. I could use the fresh air."

"Good for you. See you later."

Parker hears the roar of the diesel engine.

"I feel like a ghost," says a British twang beside her.

43

"I'm sorry?" Parker turns around. This time she notices his fingerless gloves and pin-striped vest under the ratty coat. *Definitely not a townie.* She's still holding the Tampax, which she quickly reshelves.

"You looked at me like you seen a ghost."

"Sorry, that was just, you know, a close call." Parker feels color flooding back into her face. "I mean, I wasn't expecting to see anyone I know in here. I didn't know who you were."

He laughs gruffly. "Can't tell if you're disappointed or what. Should I, like, be insulted?" When he says *like*, it sounds like *loik*. His *what* is shortened to *whuh*.

Parker thanks the guy for his help as they walk outside and stand under the gray sky. He extends one of his hands. "Jamie Drake."

"Parker," she says, shaking it. "Cole."

"Wellington, I presume," he adds, unwrapping a lollipop and shoving it in his mouth. "You want one?"

"Sure," she says, smiling *almost* shyly. Parker's not exactly the mute soul she used to be. "Green apple, please."

"Myself, I'm just blowing through town. Well, not quite. I guess I'm staying for a spell."

"Where at?" Parker asks, removing her Blow Pop to speak.

"Dear friend of the family. Old bloke named George. Over on White Oak Street."

"And what are you doing here?"

Now he grins like a thousand suns. She'll eventually learn why, when she comes to understand the way Jamie Drake operates. "Ah, it's just such a booming little mecca of culture, this Glendon. I find it quite difficult to stay away, to be reasonable with you."

She snorts and shakes her head. "You're too funny," she says dryly.

He puts a skinny arm around her shoulders and cracks his lollipop between his teeth, evaluating her with dark brown eyes. "Want to come see my house? I won't entice you in or nothing. I'll just drive you by. So you know where I am. Unless you still need the *fresh air* or whatever."

Parker gets a shiver—not of fear, not of excitement, but of *feeling*. She has a notion that she already knows him. This sequence—the gas station, the lollipop, the white sky, the stranger—is like a dream she's already had, and she recognizes all of it.

"Come *on*," he goads.

She smiles ruefully, knowing this is mad. The moment reminds her of this past summer, when she and Pete hitchhiked with an old man in a '66 Chevy pickup. They squeezed into the front, and she and Pete exchanged looks, since they'd been forbidden to do this. But the guy offered them pickles from a glass jar, and turned up Gram Parsons on the old radio, and suddenly the three of them were best friends, driving down the highway in the July heat. Parker thought of that afternoon as a touchstone of freedom, of life.

"Sure," she says.

He starts to walk her across the lot and she stops. "My skis," she says, turning around to get them.

He pretends to be shocked and dismayed. "Bloody hell, Parker Cole. If I'd known you had so much bloody baggage I might not have invited you."

Jamie drives a Mercedes G-Class, silver with black leather seats pocked with cigarette burns. It looks to Parker like a WWII vehicle, sinister and exact. Inside is a mess of wire connected to an iPhone, a McDonald's bag on the floor and ketchup packets strewn there too, and a guitar case in the backseat. He peels out, looking for a song, his eyes— under the porkpie hat and his stringy black bangs—flicking from the white road to the iPhone and back. Parker twirls her hair in the passenger seat, strangely peaceful, as if she knew where they were going.

He's ugly. Examined clinically, he's ugly. But in those brown eyes is a kid whose soul is fresh from the bath, ripe from playing in the sun, unjudged as yet, undone.

White Oak is grand and quiet, none of the houses visible from the road. Jamie skids into his driveway, Parker bracing herself. The platinum jeep comes face-to-face with a brick mansion whose doorway is flanked by Corinthian columns. Its red is the only color in the landscape against black trees and white snow.

But Jamie goes past the house, under an archway of trees to a pool house. There's a deep vacant space in the yard, which Parker assumes is the pool. Raw wood stakes with orange plastic ribbons mark its corners. Jamie puts the jeep in park and keeps it running for the heat. Parker gets goose bumps, because she's not supposed to be here.

"That's where the big man George lives," he says, jerking his thumb at the front house. "And little old me, I live up here. By my lonesome."

Parker doesn't know how to ask, and he can tell.

"My parents are in Hong Kong," he says. "I think."

"For how long?" she asks, wide-eyed.

He shrugs. "A year or two. Who the bloody hell knows?"

Parker smiles. He looks down and fiddles with his glove, unraveling the wool.

"You're an orphan," she says.

"Technically, no," he answers, still looking away. "George, there, he's the guardian of the hour."

They both turn to the mansion and see George standing at a window. He seems to be wearing a Japanese robe, and has a blur of long gray hair. He disappears and the window is a void.

"I guess you can come up," Jamie says without as much bravado as before. "I know I said you wouldn't."

"I shouldn't," Parker says firmly and gently. "I have to get back."

"I'll drive you."

"Drive me to Lakeside Road, would you? I'll catch the trail from there."

He plays his music loudly, crestfallen. Or nervous. He reminds Parker of a peacock. All his slang and swagger is an iridescent tail he puts up for courting or fighting. A fan of trickery, a shield. But here she catches him falter, and he lets his tail fold and drag in the dust. A regular bird.

As she's getting out, they look at each other. This would be the time to say they'll see each other again, or trade numbers. But they don't. Parker smiles her smile, auburn hair spilling from her fur hat, kohl-rimmed eyes crinkling in gratitude. She closes the door.

Skiing through the woods, as the light fails and branches become one with the twilight, Parker shakes her head. *So many strays this winter.*

5

The school gets a reality check at the beginning of February. The shadow of a noose hangs across the prep-school community.

The headmaster's house is in a clearing of woods. The lake is frozen, opaque like quartz. The afternoon shows no sun, the sky evenly white. The snow-covered hedges and trellises in the yard gleam.

Greg's and Delia's arms are linked, and she pulls his midnight-blue ski cap down over his eyes when the urge to tease him strikes. He leaves giant footprints from his Timberlands. Chase and Gabriel make lewd birdcalls that echo, their bare hands stuffed into coat pockets.

"What's this thing for again?" Greg asks, turning back

to consult his boys, his arm still thrown over Delia's parka-clad back.

"It's a keg party, son," Chase tells him, breaking branches.

"Some kind of announcement about what happened at Andover," Gabriel corrects.

A bird caws, screeching through trees, its wings spread in insult. The bird doesn't want them here. They stamp on the steps of the majestic house. The inside radiates warmth and sugar. When they walk in and hang their coats, and see fire crackle, and smell ginger cake and Earl Grey tea, they get congested with home-sadness. Home*sick*ness faded last year. It's been replaced by something weaker, something diluted by resignation. They have left home for good.

"Now we're in the belly of the beast," Chase whispers with mock solemnity as they make their way past tartan couches, Federal card tables, and eighteenth-century oil portraits.

"Yooo, kids," Nikki says, as the crew drifts her way.

She's seated on the hearth, sucking on a red stirrer, her fingernails a vampy purple.

Delia sits down and brushes Nikki's hair away from her face. "Hi, baby."

"Christ, your hands are cold." Nikki smiles.

Chase perches on the arm of the sofa. He gazes around the room. The headmaster and his wife chat with students, and piano music murmurs from the corner. Candy canes are slanted in a vase, and blue-blazered shoulders touch, side by side, at the hot-chocolate urn, and Chase feels almost at home. Not home, exactly, but a powerful substitute. Students rarely come to this house, and everyone becomes more likable here. As if some ghost of a mother is tucking their bangs behind their ear, or a father is clapping a hand on their knee.

"This should be morbid," Nikki says.

"I hope so," Delia answers.

Chase sees Parker standing by the sideboard, examining sweets. Wide-legged tweed pants, a black turtleneck, and black eyeliner make her look like a Paris bohemian circa 1965. She picks a cookie studded with a candied cherry. Chase looks away. *Come on over here and abuse me, will you, Park? Matter of fact, why don't you sew my ear to my chest so I have to listen to my heartbeat accelerate with anger, or something like it, every time I see you. I mean, it's only been seven months since we broke up. Never heard of water under the bridge? No? It's an interesting concept; you should look it up.* Chase takes a deep breath. *Jesus, I have issues.*

"Parks," Nikki calls, in her interfering way. "Get your ass over here."

Delia cracks up because Nikki suddenly remembers she's in the headmaster's domicile and covers her mouth.

"I mean, please come *hither*," Nikki says more loudly to be funny.

Parker saunters to them, pretending to be involved in her cookie. She sits on the hearthstone and avoids Chase's eyes.

Esther Grange, student body president, stands to speak. She's tall with dark eye circles and dishwater-blond hair. The room gets hushed.

There was another suicide last week, this one at Andover. That makes five suicides at top prep schools in the past year. This is a record high, and a *Vanity Fair* article just came out on the previous deaths. They cite the usual culprits: stress to achieve, lack of parenting and affection, drive to get into the right colleges and attain high scores. They blame the increase on the fact that these elite schools are now more merit based than before, and less legacy oriented, with smarter kids vying for the same few places at Ivy Leagues as ever. The pressure cooker got turned up.

"I don't want to talk about this article as much as I want to talk about our community," she says, already a good politician. She uses index cards, and her gold bracelets jangle. "Personally, I feel like I have *plenty* of people here to turn to if I feel down. And I go to them *before* it all starts to feel overwhelming. Do you guys know what I mean?"

"You mean you turn to them *after* you make a few notches on your inner thigh with your Swiss Army knife, and *before* you binge on Milky Ways and popcorn," Nikki amends under her breath, sending her posse into paroxysms of coughing.

While Esther drones on in her faux-comrade tone, the room is silent. Nikki takes Parker's hand, as if in friendship. She bounces Parker's palm on her own palm. But then suddenly she takes it and makes Parker touch Chase's knee. Both Parker and Chase recoil, and the room turns to the commotion. Delia snorts like a pig, trying to stifle laughter.

Esther falters. The headmaster glares.

"Sorry," Nikki whispers shakily, trying so hard to resist laughter she is almost crying.

It's so juvenile. But that's Nikki. And Parker and Chase do catch each other's look. Chase rolls his eyes, and Parker smiles. She frowns quickly, and keeps her face stern for the duration.

Do not let him in, Parker Cole, she tells herself. *Think how he has hurt you. Remember.* She sees a slide show: Chase slow-dancing with Schuyler under a disco ball, Parker swimming with him in starlight, those days at the infirmary—lying side by side in beds, walking in autumn woods while the sun burned on the lake. And then the day Laine appeared in her blue coat, returning like a virus. And Chase's heart pounding in his eyes like a cartoon. *Screw him,* she thinks now, her bitterness regained.

Laine crunches across snow topped with ice. With each step, she thinks: *This is stupid this is stupid this is stupid.*

She's meeting Noah at Happer Pond, as he humiliated her into agreeing to a skating lesson. They'd been sitting on the indigo-blue couch at the headmaster's meeting when he'd started in on how she'd be a skater if she stopped being afraid to fall.

"Gee, thanks, Buddha-master coach," she'd quipped.

"What, are you too proud to skate with me?"

No. Laine Hunt is too proud to admit that she's too proud to try something.

She sees him cresting the hill now. His skates clank, hanging by the laces from his big hand. But when he gets close, he grins, dimples deepening. His black coat has gold buttons like a funeral marching band uniform.

She's dreading this.

She cannot figure out where Noah's interest has come from. He was always the New York boy telling sordid tales no one believed. Noah seemed like Chase's desperate brother. Every prank had to be weirder. Every joke had to be told more than once. And now, all of a sudden, his eyes are directed at her this semester. *Does he want what Chase had?*

"Hey, kid," he says.

"Hey."

"I ain't gonna bite." He laughs. *Unless, of course, you're into that. I'm into anything you are. Oh, God, stop thinking.* Noah's having mental Tourette's.

"I'm not *afraid* of you," she lies.

He sweeps snow off a stone bench. She smirks at his politesse and roughly unlaces her boots. She doesn't need a benefactor.

"Ready?" he asks.

They waddle down the bank on their blades like penguins, and Noah pushes off land onto ice. He turns.

"I'm coming," she says petulantly, and stays put.

Noah does an Ice Capades twirl.

"All right, hit the ice, Hunt."

Laine skids onto the ice, which is bumpy with frozen bubbles.

"No straight legs," he says.

"I know. Gravity, et cetera, right?"

"And just glide. Push away, push to the side, not behind you."

"Yeah, I know," Laine says.

Noah watches, smiling. When he was little, his family would skate at Wollman, an outdoor rink in Central Park. His sisters buzzed around other skaters like bees. And his mom and dad skated leisurely, cashmere coats rippling, groping for each other's hand. His father cursed in French when he stumbled: *Merde, oh la!* They were like teenagers.

"Swing your arms," Noah commands.

"Swing your own arms," Laine says, and even she has to laugh at how stupid that sounds.

"Give me your hand," he says.

She glares.

"For Christ's sake, just give me your hand," he says.

"Why?"

"I'm going to show you how to swing your arms."

She holds out her mitten. He slows her down and lengthens her stride by slowing and lengthening his own stride. They skate until she doesn't have to try; it just happens. He sings Jethro Tull in a phony baritone: "Skating away, skating a-*way*! On the thin ice of a new da-a-ay."

For a few minutes, she forgets herself. He looks sideways at her and smiles.

Shit. What goes up must come down. They've had too much fun. She seems too happy. He'll be encouraged. Anne always asks Laine why she panics, why she thinks guys want so much from her. *Because they do.* Like now. Noah thinks they've gotten closer today. Their joined mittens are an agreement, the wool sealed in wax like a treaty. She takes her hand back. They climb off the pond.

"Noah," she says as they unlace their skates on the bench, the sky darkening, birds settled into the horizon.

"Yeah?" he says, happy.

"I, um. I need to say that we're just friends." There. She said it.

He stops working on his boot. Looks up, pink cheeked,

and dumbfounded with disappointment.

Laine prods: "Do you understand?"

He's insulted now. "Of course I understand."

They walk back in silence. Noah is caught in memories of failure. He grew up comfortable with girls because of his older sisters. But he never could cross that line from friends to something else. He remembers one rainy day in Manhattan, watching a herd of girls leave Nightingale, a private school near his apartment. He was maybe twelve, and alone. The girls were in drab uniforms, and looked at him with doleful eyes from under their rainbow of umbrellas. *Come on, Noah, say something. Talk to us. Cat got your tongue? Are you afraid of us? Huh? Are you scared?* He couldn't make his mouth answer, and the girls moved on, exchanging amused glances, raindrops splashing like silver as their rubber boots marched up Fifth Avenue.

When Laine and Noah near the main building door, Chase comes out of the building. Noah hesitates. Laine pauses also, but it's too late. The air crackles with discomfort.

"Well, well. Where y'all been?" Chase is bundled in his camel-hair coat. His iPod earphones dangle from his neck. Madras pants, wrong for the season, drag in the snow.

"We were just skating," Noah says, wiping his nose with his mitten.

"You guys make a cute team. Sort of a brother-sister skating combo." Chase plugs his earphones back in. "I'm just kidding."

"Whatever, dude. We're going to dinner. Want to come?"

"Think I'll pass," Chase says too quickly. "But thanks."

"Your call," Noah says.

Oh, dear Lord, Laine thinks. *Like roosters. Their chests puffed out and tails spread. News flash: I don't belong to either of you, so there's nothing to fight over.*

"I like your outfit," Noah jibes Chase as they move past each other.

"Ha-*ha,*" Chase says, smiling reluctantly.

But he stops smiling when he sees Laine's face. For a second, she looks at Noah. Her blue eyes have a speck of something. Something Chase doesn't like.

Parker *really* likes film class. The films are screened in the auditorium, twice a week in case you miss one. It's luxurious: sitting in an almost empty room, the film crackling. Parker might be alone today; she doesn't see anyone in the gloom.

Metropolis, from the 1920s, takes place in 2027. It was a faraway date when they made the iridescent story. The skyscrapers of a dystopia loom, and the faces of workers are creamy with fatigue and sooty with toil. A female robot dances in a nightclub. Children are drowned. It's weird, this old movie about the future.

When Parker stands up, in her leopard pants and Rocky's Skate Shop hoodie, she's unsteady, overwhelmed by this other world. The door at the end of the auditorium lets in the light. She squints.

"Hi," Chase says next to her.

She jumps, puts a hand on her heart.

"Did I scare you?" he asks in a jaded tone.

She doesn't have time to assemble all her hatred. "Hi," she says.

Maybe he senses a window. "Parker. Can we, if not become friends, can we at least not be enemies?" he asks tiredly.

She feels foolish, and shrugs. "Yeah."

He makes an amazed face. "That was too easy."

"What? I said we won't be enemies. I didn't say we'd be friends." She tries to look indifferent.

But he smiles as he backs away, like he just won something. She watches as he turns to walk forward, into the white glare. His golden hair. Those wide scarecrow shoulders. His dirty Southern strut.

"Shit," she says to herself.

She leaves the main building, walking blindly. *Argghh! This is infuriating.* She's traumatized. Anyone eavesdropping wouldn't know it was a big deal, considering the conversation took less than a minute. But to Parker it took hours, and encyclopedias were communicated. She could analyze every particle of it, his motives, tone, body language, the message inside the message.

The stone foyer of Gray smells of wool and snow. The problem is that she can't take Chase lightly. A minor interaction leaves her demoralized, or weak with a stupid hopefulness—and for what?

"Parker." Mrs. Jenkins stops her on the stairs. "I need to talk to you."

"Okay." Parker follows the reddish bob down the hall, not liking the tone of her voice. Her heart falls an inch in her rib cage.

Mrs. Jenkins stands at her front door. A wreath of pepper berry hangs, thorny like Jesus' crown. From within, the perfume of candles and Russian tea.

"What is it, Mrs. Jenkins?" Parker asks.

Mrs. Jenkins opens the door, and the dog comes out, his tail wagging so hard his body undulates. A bandage binds his hind leg; his scars are black, but his eyes are aquamarine. He comes straight to Parker and sniffs her pants, snuffing the hems as if he can't get enough.

"Oh my God," is all Parker can manage, over and over, and she sinks down onto the floor. The dog licks her face, and she giggles.

"You have to name him," Mrs. Jenkins says.

"I can't believe this," Parker says, looking up with gratitude that overwhelms the teacher. Parker tries not to cry, pressing her face to his spine. "I don't even know what to say."

"He's going to stay with me. And I'm going to hold you to your promise to work him out. He's a strong guy; he needs exercise."

"Oh my God, I'll totally do that, no problem."

Parker looks into the dog's eyes. She can't *believe* that Mrs. Jenkins is doing this, taking him in so Parker can be near him. She'll name him Moses, whose father ordered his death in the bulrushes, but who was not meant to die. She wants to get him a crimson collar with gold studs. He's gonna be a punk-rock dog.

6

Wednesday afternoon. Everyone else has a game, but Parker's in her room, doodling Moses in an art pad. They spent the past half hour throwing a stick in the icy field; that's all his back leg could take, according to the vet, so Parker returned him to Mrs. Jenkins. She sketches his face, an old cowboy rag around his neck. Him jumping through a hoop of fire.

Moses can't save her from the work, though. All these books and notebooks could line a padded cell. She's behind in calculus and physics, as well as music history—even though she loves music. She hasn't practiced for the SAT, either, because those ovals offend her.

This semester is already more than she can handle, and she's been having anxiety attacks. She thinks of that Taiwanese girl at Andover who hanged herself with her roommate's Anne Klein belt. A teddy bear was on the floor, and they think she was holding it. She was an Upper-form too, and among her straight A's was one B-plus for Medieval English.

Her teacher had been interviewed on the news. "She came to me crying, said she had to get an A. She needed to get into MIT. She was furious. Well," the woman said, her face trembling, "I guess I don't understand how it could matter so much that she took her life."

That same teacher was probably part of the pressure to get A's. It's the forked-tongue message: *Everything matters, but don't let it matter too much.*

When the room phone rings, she looks at it with disdain. She was liking her privacy. She was kind of enjoying wallowing in anxiety and pity.

"Hello?"

"Bloody hell," the voice says.

"Who is this?" she says, her voice cracking into a smile. *How did he find me?*

"The operator didn't want to give me your number. I had to tell her you were my sis. She's like your mum, eh? Fussy little bird."

Parker laughs. "Stricter than my mother."

"Come over."

"What?"

"I'll come get you."

"You can't do that."

"Why not?"

Parker pictures him on his bed, hat twirling on finger, wing-tip shoes marking his sheets.

"Because if they see me leave with you, they'll need to know you," she says. "I need permission to be picked up in a car."

"Walk a ways. I'll come get you at the intersection of Canon and Linden, then."

She laughs. He won't give up. "Okay."

As she tramps through snow, she feels a thrill. She's getting *away*, slipping through the claws of the dragon. She swaggers. She's going to a stranger's house. The Mercedes is waiting, smoke chugging from its exhaust pipe. As Parker opens the door and hops up, he smiles and she smiles back. Old friends.

They skid up the long drive. The main house's top story is lit. They curve around to the pool house and get out. She looks at the void that is the pool, and imagines summertime. Strangers drinking lemonade and lying on the stones, a shirt over their eyes, as June bugs spin in chlorinated water and roses bloom. The bottom floor of the pool house is dark, and she can just see piles of lemon-yellow-and-white-striped cushions for the recliners through the windows.

"After you," Jamie says.

He's got courage: a strange actor on a stage alone. Like a

mime trying to get the saddest kid to smile.

She walks up the stairs and smells stale smoke and Pledge. When she reaches the top, she looks around the efficiency. One wall is lined with chrome shelves, a Sub-Zero fridge, a Viking range. The counters are black marble. His bed is made with a French coverlet, with a bolster tied like a Tootsie Roll at both ends. What a funny place for Jamie to lay his greasy head. On the floor, magazines from Italy, Prague, Australia. Sandalwood incense. A vintage pair of white leather ankle boots.

"My bachelor pad," he says, sweeping his long skinny arm.

"By the way," she says now, "I'm just here to hang out. Not to do anything—"

He holds up a hand. "Bollocks! I thought we might dress as American Gladiators and pummel one another. Guess I'm out of luck."

Parker laughs and sits.

"Speak no more, love," Jamie says, flashing that mega-bright smile. "We're agreed. I've got really, *really* good intentions."

They smoke, lying on the floor and watching footage on Jamie's computer; he's found the David Letterman from the late eighties with Crispin Glover tripping on acid. It's hysterical and creepy. They light new cigarettes. Using one hand to type, since her smoke is in the other hand, Parker shows him a YouTube video of Robbie Williams falling off the stage in Germany.

Once they're done laughing, he turns over to lie on his back, and sighs. "Oh, hell."

"What is it?" Parker asks.

His face is in profile, his skin white and pitted. His eyes are closed, and his black hair sticks to his head. He looks like a rock star in a coma. But then he opens his eyes, and his face becomes charming. "Fuck all, Park, I was about to"– and here he twirls his fingers around and whistles–"spiral, if you know what I mean. I'm glad you came over. This afternoon is just *dark*."

"Well, I'm glad you came and got me."

He turns on his side, head perched in the cup of his hand. "Tell me something about you."

"What should I tell you?"

He shakes his head dreamily. "Anything. I don't give a fucking hell what. Tell me where you were born, or why they named you Parker. Tell me about getting your first period. Tell me you killed someone."

"O-*kaayyy*. Let's see." She thinks. "I'll tell you a memory. It's just a vague memory. I was six, and I remember this guy staying with our family for, like, a week. We had set up a room in our house but he wanted to stay in the barn. He was in his sixties, right? And totally, completely out there. My father knew him from Oregon. The whole time the guy was there, my dad was out of his tree."

"Just crazy?"

"No, crazy drinking, crazy on drugs."

"You knew that then?"

"Well, I felt it. Later I understood better. Because my dad's sober now. I guess he decided at some point the stuff wasn't for him, although for my really young years he was pretty loopy, unpredictable. Anyway, I go into the barn one day, looking for my cat. And my dad and this guy have strung up these wires across the barn, right? And hanging from them are seashells, wind chime pipes, soda bottles, seedpods, and all kinds of stuff. They explained how they were creating an organic piano or something, but I just left them alone."

Jamie beams. "That's off the grid."

"Guess who the guy was?" Parker says, stubbing out her cigarette.

"Tell me."

"Ken Kesey."

"Bollocks!" Jamie says exuberantly. "No way! Ken Kesey is your godfather?"

"I didn't say *that*."

"Yeah, but I'm trying to show you how to make your story better, little girl."

"Wasn't it good enough?" she asks, somewhat playfully.

At this, he stops, and does look at her. "You *are* good enough, Miss Parker."

Then he jumps up and sits on the couch, starts fumbling with a silver box studded with turquoise and red stones. She rises to sit next to him. He pulls out a prescription bottle.

"Want some candy?"

"What is it?"

"Vicodin. Sure to banish the demons."

She doesn't hesitate. She'll look back at this moment and wonder why she didn't pause. "Sure."

He breaks it in half. "You'll barely feel it, luvvy. It'll just airbrush out the stains and splotches; you know what I'm saying, yeah?"

She swallows it with Diet Coke, and they chitchat, and she pretends not to be monitoring effects. Parker's never taken a prescription drug. She's nervous.

When it's time to go, a half hour later, they get in the car with a rare camaraderie. It's a bond that happens when both people know they're liked by the other. Despite this, though, driving through fog, Parker knows Jamie doesn't necessarily want to kiss her. He acts afraid of brushing against her. When she steps out, he doesn't say anything. He puts a hand to his cap. He's a mystery.

She thought the pill didn't make her feel anything. But walking alone, past a house with a neat pillow of snow on its roof and a gray cat posing by a jade plant in the dark window, she feels it all. It's beautiful. Her soul is hushed, the silence profound, like when a baby stops crying. On top of that, she's high on rebellion. *Welcome to Wonderland, Parker Cole.*

Laine gets out of the cab and approaches Anne's office in the Glendon Medical Services building. She's slightly dreading talking to Anne about Noah. The outside is yellow brick with chrome railings, but the room is cozy. Sun pools on the floor, and trees shadow the walls. A cobalt-blue bowl is stacked with tangerines. Anne has black hair streaked white, wide skirts like a farmer's wife or an old hippie, and silver bracelets.

"So that's excellent," Anne says, sitting in an armchair. "You're letting yourself fall down, and you're having fun. You wouldn't have done that last year."

"I wouldn't have, no way," Laine agrees. They're talking about hockey. "Noah helped with the skating part, for sure."

"How *is* Noah?" Anne asks now.

"It's just friendship. I mean, I think he might like me. But I'm not interested in him. He's always been the 'other guy,' you know? Greg is the athlete, Chase is the rock star, and Gabriel is mysterious. I always thought Noah was the redheaded stepchild."

"Is he like Chase with you, or different?"

"Umm." Laine looks at the ceiling. Laine has explained how Chase wanted to open her, like a rag doll. Spill her stuffing. He seemed to love her, but wanted to take her apart. It wasn't exciting. It was frightening. Noah *is* different. "Noah's a little more the caretaking sort."

"Is he physically affectionate with you?" Anne asks.

Laine lets Anne ask her mortifying questions. At first, Laine felt uncomfortable with this stranger. But her stepfather demanded Laine see someone. Anne is amazing; instead of listening with indifference, she's affected. Her eyes welled up when Laine was describing 60 Thompson, the cocaine, the orchids in the hall, seeing her bloody face in the mirror.

"He is, a little bit."

"Does it bother you, or do you like it?"

"Sometimes it bothers me," Laine admits.

Anne and Laine have discussed the lack of affection or intimacy in her family. No one ever said, "I love you." There was little hugging, and it was formal. When Laine's mom, Polly, put her to bed, she would pat Laine's head and say: *Mommy gives you a kiss.* But never kiss her.

But the divorce broke her parents. They were raised to dream, conceive, and achieve, and then they'd failed the precious job: family. Anne helped Laine see her parents as human beings, not enemies, and herself and her sisters as willful and alive, not victims. It took Anne to make Laine see heartbreak in that house. And so when Polly kissed Laine over Christmas, her eyes wet, Laine didn't wince. She looked instead with amazement at her mother.

Before the session is over, Anne asks why Laine is hanging out with Noah, if she's not interested in him.

"Yeah, we hang out," Laine says. "But just as friends."

"And you're not afraid you're stringing him along?"

"Well, I don't know," she answers, flustered.

"Are you sure you don't feel anything for him?"

"What do you mean, 'feel anything'?" Laine asks.

But time is up, and they say good-bye, Anne's bracelets jingling as she rubs Laine's back and opens the door.

Walking Moses on Friday, Parker has no reason to suspect that this day will lead her down a previously unimaginable path.

Parker picks up her puppy after class, and he jumps on her, front paws heavy with strength, his face twisted in a smile. She snaps the leash onto his collar.

"Come on, boy. Let's go, mister."

They walk into the gray day, and Moses crisscrosses the path. He's proud to walk with his mother. He knocks snow with his nose to get at smells buried under drifts. He melts the white with golden piss.

Every so often, he looks back as if to ask: *How we doing? We doing okay?* She brings dining hall Cheerios in her coat pocket as rewards for heeling and sitting.

After the walk, Mr. Jenkins opens the door. Moses gallops clumsily to the water bowl.

"He's a good boy, isn't he?" Mr. Jenkins asks, hands in the pockets of his corduroys.

"Yeah. After the hard life he started out with, he's still trusting. It seems almost unnatural."

"Or profoundly natural. You did save him."

Mrs. Jenkins comes into the room, reading glasses on. "Parker, I have an interesting proposal for you."

After listening, Parker laughs at the idea, but Mrs. Jenkins tells her to give it a try. Parker's never done anything like this.

Now it's the next day, and she has to follow through. She stands in one wing of the stage, unfamiliar with the velvet curtain, the dust, the pages and bright lights. Jorgen and Susie read the balcony scene. Jorgen reads Romeo with a Swedish accent, but she can see him as an Italian teenager in lust, noble and doomed.

Parker reads with Arden. Mrs. Jenkins and her assistant, Toby, sit in the fourth row with legal pads and pencils. Parker auditions for the Nurse—because it seems unassuming. Parker clears her throat.

"'What, lamb! what, ladybird!
God forbid! Where's this girl?'"

It's strange, what happens here that didn't happen when

practicing yesterday in her room. Slowly, as if growing layers, she turns into the Nurse. Clothes blossom on her like petals: an apron, a bonnet, long skirts, bell sleeves. She says:

"'I'll lay fourteen of my teeth,–/And yet, to my teeth be it spoken, I have but four–/She is not fourteen.'"

And she feels her teeth fall out. Parker stands on the stage after they finish, exquisitely embarrassed, stripped of costume and in her birthday suit.

"That was great, guys," Mrs. Jenkins says, marking her page without pleasure or disapproval. "Arden, thanks. Parker, can you read Juliet, with Gerald? We don't have any girls in the wings."

"Um, sure," Parker says.

Gerald is a short kid from a Vermont farm. He rolls plaid shirtsleeves to get down to the business of Shakespeare: "'Have not saints lips, and holy palmers too?'"

Mrs. Jenkins calls from the dark seats: "He wants to kiss you, Park. And you're being coy."

Parker registers that, and says: "'Ay, pilgrim, lips that they must use in prayer.'"

Mrs. Jenkins says: "Gerald, you come back at her."

Gerald says: "'O, then, dear saint, let lips do what hands do/ They pray, grant thou, lest faith turn to despair.'"

Parker says: "'Saints do not move, though grant for prayers' sake.'" She feels like she *is* flirting. She transforms—an insect breaking from its chrysalis—into Juliet.

Gerald says: "'Then move not while my prayer's effect I take./ Thus from my lips, by thine, my sin is purg'd.'"

"And this is where you would kiss her," Mrs. Jenkins says.

Gerald and Parker look at each other. This is where they draw the line.

Chase is standing in the back row. He came to try out because somewhere in his mind he believes he's Johnny Depp. Or because it would be something to do while Greg necked with Delia in the student center and Gabriel chased around his new crush, Seiko. At the very least, it would be better than watching snow fall, or his cigarette burn.

But this makes him sick, Gerald leering at Parker. She's a head taller, the ivory Tibetan beads clacking on her wrist as she raises her long arm, and in a different league than this pipsqueak. *Screw this*. He doesn't feel like being Romeo after all. Why is she everywhere he wants to be? The school is too small. He throws the script in the garbage as he storms out. This hurts, as he's not one to be crowded out of his rightful place. *He* doesn't get kicked off the island.

Noah's in his own hell. Wherever he goes, Laine appears and vanishes, like a fever dream, a mirage from sun hitting snow. He walks through force fields of her, as if she'd been condensed into beads of ice or oxygen. He takes off his sunglasses, rubs the lenses on his shirt. Tries to see straight.

The whole thing makes him ill. He sucks down Pepto-Bismol like mother's milk. When he sees her in chapel, in the flesh, the floor becomes unsteady, like the deck of a ship.

Noah's lovesick.

7

Deep winter. The waterfalls are stalled; white beards hang from black rocks. Plows have shoved snow so high onto shoulders that parked cars are buried to their windows, like toys in a sandbox. A film of snow makes the pavement slimy.

Chase is walking to chapel with two nerds from his floor. The snow sends pink and orange spangles into the air, snowflakes caught like sequins in his lashes. He's feeling down and he just can't get up. Yesterday at squash practice, his coach asked if his feet were made of lead. *They feel like they are, in fact, sir, yes.*

Parker's entering chapel as Chase takes his seat in the wooden pew. She casts him a cold glance, as usual. He's been fuming since he abandoned that audition last week.

He didn't need or even want to be in the play. But it makes him nuts he can't be in the same room as Parker. She said they aren't enemies; why can't she smile? Is it that hard to smile?

"Good morning, students!" says Mr. Bloom, the Dean of Theology. "Today we're going to start with the choral group."

As kids sing, Chase makes a decision. After the rows of pews are released into the marble hall, he zooms in. Parker sees him in her peripheral vision, as she always does. His trademark untucked burgundy turtleneck and hand-me-down sports coat. Honey-blond hair in his sleepy eyes.

"Hey, Park. I've been looking for you." He's got that wry, fallen-prince smile. "Can we, um, talk?"

"I'm sorta busy right now, Chase."

"That's cool," he says, lazily scratching his head as if they talk every day. "Maybe later today? We could cruise out to one of the cabins. And just, like, hash it out and stuff."

"Well," she says, thinking. A diabolical idea crosses her mind. A way to make him jealous. *Chase—jealous. Imagine that.* Chase, who walked into this school and made ten best friends within the hour. Chase, who moves easily through social ranks, even with ennui, whereas Parker gets stuck. She has something he doesn't have. An exit. A place off campus. A friend on the outside. "I'm going over to this friend's place. He lives in Glendon."

Chase shrugs. "Are you inviting me? Is he, like, cool with that?"

"I wasn't exactly inviting you," Parker says.

"*Sweet*, you're too generous. Is he your boyfriend or something?"

Now Parker's face twists—with sadistic pleasure at the question, and with genuine discomfort. Some girls can play good games; Parker's not one of them. "Not really."

"I got squash, but I could pull a Sports Red Card."

Parker's turn to shrug. "Do it, if you want."

Chase meets Parker later at the Glendon taxi behind her dorm—he just wants to pursue this absurd venture. A field trip with Parker, his ex-girlfriend, who hates him. It's almost funny. The wind blows her hair, and she pulls her rabbit-fur jacket tight. She's in shock. She didn't *really* expect him to show up. She feels like she won in some way. Dirty Diane, the cantankerous cabbie, is behind the wheel.

"So what disease did you catch?" Parker asks, too shy to look at him.

"Diarrhea. It's my go-to." Chase ducks to get into the cab in his faded Levi's and a hunter-green V-neck cashmere sweater. "It's genius. No one questions it, and the nurses can't get you out the door fast enough."

"Pleasant. Thanks for sharing." Parker rolls her eyes.

It's practically balmy for midwinter. When Dirty D drops Parker and Chase at the red house, they make arrangements to get picked up. Chase thanks D for keeping this "between them," winking like an adulterous senator, and tips her big.

Jamie Drake is poolside on a recliner. In skinny jeans, a peacoat, and Wayfarer sunglasses, he looks like he just survived a hard night in a Chateau Marmont bungalow, not a boring afternoon in the Connecticut sticks. On the foot of his lounger, a girl in a gunnysack dress with leg warmers plays with her iPhone. Chase thinks she looks homeless, but beautiful. She can't hide it.

"Hullo, mates!" Jamie waves dully. "Parker, who's your friend?"

"This is Chase. I hope you don't mind."

"Of course not. Chase, I'm Jamie, and this little lassie is Sophie."

Sophie reaches to the ashtray in the snow for her lit cigarette and looks up at the guests. In her oversize sunglasses, it's hard to tell if she's even looking at Parker and Chase. She takes a drag. "Pleasure."

"So, what are you all up to?" Parker asks, off-kilter to find a houseguest.

"We're fixing to do laps, what's it look like, luv?" Jamie says.

"Actually, we're about to eat acid." Sophie sneers. "You got here just in time."

Acid? Chase was expecting townies, middle-class kids

chugging Midori in a dark garage and blasting Linkin Park. Usually, Chase has no problem hanging with the older crowd. He grew up the little brother, the one sent to do the dirty work. *Hey, Chase, shut the door. Hey, Chase, go ask that girl for her number. Hey, Chase, chug this beer. Tell Mom and Dad I got home by eleven. Don't tell Mom and Dad I puked on the front lawn. Don't say anything at all.* But he smells bigger trouble at the pool house.

"She's just messing around, fella," Jamie says. "Here, take a Genesee."

He twists a beer from the six-pack wedged into the snow and tosses it. As Chase pops the can, he looks at the main house.

"Don't sweat it. The benefactor isn't home."

"Seriously, Chase, relax." Parker can't resist the jab, as she opens her own Genesee. "So, where *is* George?"

"Big George is in Thailand."

"Vacation?" Parker asks.

"Something like that. Listen, why don't we head up to the flat, yeah?" Jamie asks.

They clomp upstairs, Sophie weaving in a glamorous way, her cigarette held high above her blond head so the smoke rises. The apartment is in the same condition as when Parker was last here. The only new life is a full ashtray on the marble counter, and silk dresses and gray jeans spilling from Sophie's suitcase.

Jamie sits at his Notebook and manages the playlist. Radiohead's "Karma Police" drones from the speakers. Sophie sits next to Parker on the bed, grabs a magazine, and pulls out her Drum to roll.

"You all have to try this hash my little Algerian friend gave me," she says, eyes narrowed at her work.

Welcome to the candy store, Chase thinks, as he sips his beer and watches her.

Sophie crumbles hash onto the tobacco, licks the paper closed, and lights up. Chase is amazed at her elegance. He's used to puffing hard on anything with THC, but Sophie nurses it, taking drags with no urgency. When the joint makes it to Parker and Chase, they imitate the casualness.

They share a glance; both of them are unnerved as well as invigorated to be getting high together, and to be in this weirdly sophisticated setting. They're allies, almost, being outsiders here.

"You want to see pics of Sophie?" Jamie points at the screen. "She's the new Edun girl. Check this out."

Sophie's in a tight white "One" tee and black tights.

"Holy shit. I thought you looked familiar," Parker says. "Is that Bono's company?"

"Yeah." Jamie grins. "Sophie's the bloody It girl and we can't do anything to save her."

"Wait, you've been in those American Apparel ads too, right?" Chase joins the conversation. Having spent months memorizing the American Apparel catalog, he feels a closeness to Sophie.

"That was a while back," Sophie says, as if speaking of something that happened in the 1950s. She takes off her sunglasses and rubs her eyes. "That's sort of how I got my start."

"Start?" Chase asks.

She looks at him with daggers. "Yeah. In modeling. My *start*."

"Sorry," he rushes to say. The hash is making him slow. And his confidence is drained in her company. He thinks of models in Miami who paid him zero attention. Chase decides to stop asking questions. The hash is sending funhouse ripples through *everyone's* self-image.

Parker, in fact, gets chatty and bombards Sophie with questions: "Is Bono really that environmentally conscious? Does he spend that much time in Africa or is it an act? Does he always wear those sunglasses?"

Chase looks around the room; it's a mecca of everything he can't get on campus. But Jamie makes him uneasy. It might be that Brit accent, which Chase thinks is exaggerated. Or the way Jamie tugs Parker's hair sometimes, as if he and Parker were old buddies. Now Jamie puts on the new Ryan Adams album and mumbles something about being at Ryan's house once, and then he plays drums to the song with two pens. *It's a lot of theater.*

But the day is about to get weirder. On Chase's third trip to the fridge he finds it empty. "Jamie, no more Genesees."

"No prob, Chaz." Jamie pops up from the bed, where he's been lying sandwiched between the two girls. "George has plenty of booze. Come wit' me, fella."

Jamie leads Chase into the main house. The hallway is dark and their footsteps are made quiet by an Afghan runner. Framed Japanese geishas line the oak walls, their faces blooming out of the gloom. Chase does a double take at the last one, a pornographic drawing of a geisha and a man.

"Whoa," he says under his breath.

In the next room, Chase catches up to Jamie, who's inspecting the liquor cabinet. Chase looks around the dark den. The furnishings are Moroccan, and an antique daybed is covered in silk quilts. A hookah stands in the corner, its tubes and mouthpieces at rest like a sleeping octopus's tentacles.

And along one wall are Bruce Weber photographs of teenaged boys, half-clothed, sunning with dogs, or swimming in dawn-lit ponds.

What goes on here?

"Come on over, Chase." Jamie is considering an emerald Tanqueray bottle. He unscrews the silver top, and then spits into the bottle. He grins at an astonished Chase. "We won't drink that one. It's George's favorite."

"Okay," Chase says, trying to laugh at the prank.

"I need to ask you something," Jamie says, rummaging.

"Go ahead."

"Do you think Sophie's hot? Like, super bloody hot?"

"Sure. I mean, she's a model, right? She's paid to be hot."

Jamie stares at Chase. "Do you want to shag her?"

"Umm, I don't know." *Is this a trick question?* "Why?"

"Just curious. She might fuck you, you know. I could talk her into it." Jamie hands Chase a bottle of Campari. "All right, let's go back upstairs, lad. Our business in the palace is done."

When they get back, Jamie pours Campari-and-sodas and says he has an announcement. "Chase told me he wants to shag our Sophie."

"Hold on. I didn't—" Chase is cut off by Sophie.

"Oh, you're not shy, are you, Chase?" she says, smiling like an angel, her eyes red and high.

Parker glares.

"Go ahead, Chase. This is a once-in-a-lifetime opportunity," Jamie encourages him.

Chase tries to make eye contact with Parker but she looks away. "Um. This is crazy." His voice has an edge. He's being made a fool of. The way his brother has always done to him. His father, too. He can almost take it from his own blood, but not this asshole.

Sophie crawls across the bed toward Chase. "Don't be

such a goody-goody." She puts her hand on his leg.

"Okay." Chase stands up. He's *pissed*. "That's it. Game over. Parker, we need to get back. The cab is coming."

"Whoa, whoa, whoa. We were just messing with you," Jamie says, putting on his hat as if suddenly vulnerable.

Sophie lies back down. "Don't worry, Chase. I would never have sex with you anyways."

"Much appreciated," Chase says, as he gathers up his and Parker's coats. *That bitch.*

Parker is looking at Chase, dumbfounded by his initiative. She stands up, lets him help her into her coat. "Are we really leaving?" she asks, her voice stoned.

"Yeah," Chase says.

Jamie follows them down the stairs. "Wait, hold on," he says.

They stand in front of the pool house, where the afternoon has turned to periwinkle dusk.

"What?" Chase asks stubbornly.

"In all seriousness, chap, I didn't mean to offend. I get bloody stupid sometimes, and play tricks. They mean nothin'. Swear to you."

Chase looks at this gangly stranger with tremulous eyes and pasty skin. The wrinkled stovepipe pants. Jamie looks like a little boy asking not to be thrown out of the game, not to be sent home, not to be excluded from the gang.

"It's cool," Chase says. "Honestly, it was excellent

coming over here. You got a nice setup, dude. I'm sure we'll be back." And he smiles. *The mentally unstable British twit does have a nice setup, and good candy.*

But zero sanity.

Jamie seems relieved. He looks at Parker.

"You mad at me, luv?" he asks.

She shakes her head. "No, you asshole."

They all laugh, and Chase and Parker leave Jamie behind, head to the cab waiting at the drive's end. Parker's dragging her boots in a comical way.

"Oh, man. I got a little fucked up," she says. "Did you?"

"Yeah," he answers. *"Wow."*

"Crazy, right?"

"Um, yeah. Fucking out of their minds."

"But better than squash practice, right?" Parker says.

"Much better, Park. Thanks for bringing me over. Seriously. Almost as much fun as puking together in the old infirmary last year."

"Nothing could be as fun as that," she says. She bumps shoulders with him, grins in that wolfish way, and takes one of his hands. Holds it in hers. Then drops it.

His heart stops but he keeps walking.

8

Noah's got an idea. This is the kind of thing he often dreams of doing but has never gone through with before. His dad called him yesterday to remind him about the wedding of James Monroe and Bridget Yardley, both of whom actually graduated from Wellington nine years ago. He races to catch up with Laine outside the hockey rink.

"Hey, Laine!"

Laine turns, slim and elegant in boot-cut cords and a North Face fleece. "Hi."

"So, I caught the end of your scrimmage," Noah says. "Not bad."

"Noah, we lost zero to eight and I got on the ice for a minute."

"Progress, Laine. Progress. I mean, you barely knew how

to skate a few weeks ago, right?"

Laine cracks a smile. "Yeah, I still can't understand why the coach actually kept me," she says.

"He must see something in you." Noah knows how corny that sounded. He changes the subject quickly: "Hey, I have to go to a wedding in Westport this weekend. My dad's godson. Should be amazing. I'd love for you to come."

Laine pauses and Noah considers making a run for it.

"Um." Anne is in her head saying that she should accept invitations. "Sure." Laine agrees against her will, against her instincts.

"Great!" Noah can't hide his surprise. "I mean, *cool*. I'll see you later, then." *HOLY SHIT!*

And even though he's starving, Noah heads toward Cadwallader instead of pushing his luck and going to the cafeteria. Progress comes at a cost.

Laine, meanwhile, moves around the salad bar, choosing tomatoes, adding feta cheese. Kicking herself for saying yes. *It's just so hard to disappoint the guy.* That's what she tells herself.

"So, what's the plan of attack on Saturday?" Greg asks.

Winter term is approaching its nadir, but there's a window of excitement. It's the Taft Rivalry weekend, when all of Wellington's teams compete against their enemy, culminating with the guys' hockey game Saturday night. Each year the schools trade hosting. This year it's Wellington's turn.

"I said, listen up, fellas!" Greg says. "What are we gonna do this year? Egg 'em again? Kidnap their mascot? Torture their women and children? What have you got?"

Greg, who just finished some Mountain Dew and Sprees, is hyper and bored. All the guys have a free period after lunch on Wednesdays and spend it at the Cadwallader common room. Chase is sprawled on a ratty couch, turtleneck untucked and Sperry shoes kicked off. Gabriel and Noah are sweating on Gabriel's Nintendo Wii: Noah as Nadal, Gabe as Federer.

"Dude, we're in a tiebreak at Wimbledon. Can we get a little silence?" Noah asks.

"Seriously, geeks, what are we doing?" Greg says.

Every year, the hosting students prank their guests. It's the one night that students get away with something, as long as no one gets hurt and there's no drinking or drugs involved. The tradition is encouraged; it's school pride. Teachers won't talk about it but they'll smile when students boast.

"We need gas masks, stink bombs, night-vision glasses, maybe some roadside IED's," Chase says. "Do we have these provisions?"

"A'ight, smart-ass, you're thinking, that's good. I know your ass will come up with some dirty shit." Greg points to Gabriel. "Gabe, any guerrilla tactics? Some maneuvers from back in the day at the estancia? Some *Traffic*-type shit?"

"I'm not at liberty to discuss that." Gabriel wipes his forehead and rubs his hand on his Armani pants.

Gabriel's so sarcastic, no one knows when he's kidding. But he should feel vengeful. Last year at Taft, Gabriel had been a casualty, knocked off his feet by Taft students with a fire hose "on loan" from the local truck. Gabriel and a few others were so cold they had to go back to Wellington before the game started.

Now he pauses the Wii and faces the guys. "Where do you think we could get our hands on a few crickets in the middle of winter?"

"Gabe, I don't even know what the fuck a cricket is, but I like it." Greg smiles. He plays the "boy from the city" card for effect. "Noah, you're logistics. Can you find some crickets?"

"Sorry, guys, count me out." Noah unpauses the game, and fires a backhand to Gabriel.

"What?" Gabriel lets the ball go by and looks at Noah. "What's more important?"

"Well, Laine and I are going to a wedding in Westport," he mumbles.

"Your coach is letting you miss the biggest game of the year?" Gabriel re-pauses the game.

"It's my father's godson. He's like family. Plus, it's not like I'm going to see the ice." Noah's answer sounds rehearsed. He pauses. "And, after Cocoa Beach, I'm not exactly interested in making more trouble. Tempting fate."

"That's messed up, man," Greg says. "Who's going to drive the getaway car?"

"Yeah, and who's going to steal my next girlfriend?" Chase asks.

A silence. No one meets anyone's eyes. Everyone knows Chase is being territorial about Laine, but not even Chase can figure out why. From day one, their relationship was lacking soul. They were together for the same reasons people buy expensive cars and watches and houses that they can't afford: because it seems like the right thing to do. The blue-eyed Greenwich heiress and the Prince of Tides, betrothed for a minute.

"She was barely ever your girlfriend," Noah finally says, scoffing.

"Fuck you, Noah," Chase drawls, half in jest.

Noah spins around and hurls his controller at Chase, hitting him in the chest. "Grow up."

Chase tries to stand but Noah's on top of him and pushes him off the couch. Greg gets between them before Chase can retaliate. They all start to laugh gruffly and uncomfortably.

"All right, chill the fuck out," Greg says. "Neither of your asses can fight worth shit."

"Sorry, dude," Noah says in a weird voice, smiling, embarrassed.

Chase looks disheveled, pale. "Totally. My bad." He's

slumped on the couch. He won't look at Greg.

Gabriel retrieves the controller and puts it on the coffee table. He clears his throat. "Anyone heading to Main Building?"

Saturday is mean and cold. New England shows what's up its sleeve. Crows fly in angry arcs. After morning classes, Chase is in his room, looking at white turrets, when he sees Parker walking her dog. He grabs his scarf and runs down the main stairs in a sweater, jeans, and swiftly pulled-on boots, unlaced.

"Park!" he shouts, and catches up while she waits. "Can I officially meet this guy?"

"This is Moses," she says, as if introducing someone of great stature.

Chase bends to pet the dog, and Moses sniffs his hands, then licks him. "You a good boy?"

"He's the best boy."

"You're like the dog whisperer," he tells her.

"Gee, thanks."

"So," Chase starts. He has a funny look, a challenge, on his face. Since that day at Jamie's, this is how they've interacted: with a *touché, fair is fair, right back at you* attitude. "You coming to the game later?"

She smiles but shakes her head. "Naw. Not in the mood," she says.

"Oh well. Your loss."

She laughs. "Yeah, my loss, I'm sure. I'll always regret not making it to the Taft-Wellington hockey game."

He smiles too. "Well, you'll be missed."

"Maybe I'll see you after," she says brazenly. "Now go back to your dorm. You'll freeze to death."

Chase blows kisses at Moses as he walks backward.

Parker kneels next to her dog and rubs her face against his neck. *So this is what it feels like to have the upper hand.*

Meanwhile, Noah and Laine are eating beef tenderloin with horseradish sauce at a Connecticut estate. Noah's in brown Prada, with hair slicked, shoes shined. Laine looks perfect with him, in her cashmere dress and spectator heels, her hair in a chignon. She was terrified of meeting his parents, as she's probably notorious from 60 Thompson. But Mirielle and Lucien beam, happy to see their son with a lovely girl.

"It's good, right?" Noah asks between bites.

"Much better than what we would be eating at the dining hall, that's for sure."

They feel like escaped convicts, decadently free, and superior to everyone they left behind. This house, the bride's family home, is majestic. Fourteen bedrooms, and grand living and dining rooms. Stables, a pond, guest cottages, woods. The sun sets through black clouds. The house twinkles with chandeliers, candles, and fires in the hearths.

Noah's sisters sit across the room with friends. Laine's intimidated. Anais is at Brown, and Colette at Barnard. Both are pretty and chic, although not conventionally beautiful. They have long, Gallic faces, deep-set eyes, and the same lengthy nose as their dad. They look like their brother. Having met them makes Laine think differently of Noah. They're all affectionate and easy with one another. It's sweet. It's what Laine never had.

James, the groom, puts his hands on Noah's shoulders. His corn-yellow hair lies in waves, like *The Great Gatsby*. "Thank you both for coming," he says ebulliently.

"It's a pleasure to be here," Laine says.

"It was a beautiful ceremony," Noah says.

"Why, thank you. I meant every word. Let's hope she did too."

They all laugh. James claps his hands on Noah's shoulders one more time and looks at Laine.

"This is a great fellow," James says.

Noah looks down, and Laine blushes, while James moves to the next table. She twirls her fork in the mashed potatoes. It feels as though the room is watching the two of them. The flower girls are chasing each other, hiding under tables, freesia in their hair. A woman wearing red lipstick next to Noah talks to someone else about studying painting in Italy. An older gentleman sits back in his chair, smiling fondly at the newlyweds.

And Noah puts his arm behind Laine's shoulders, rests it on her chair. And she likes it there.

The pranksters are watching the end of the game, clattering on the metallic bleachers as they jump and cheer with the rest of the crowd. Wellington is leading by one, thanks to a hat trick by Brian Leetch Jr., son of the Hall-of-Famer. The new William T. Wilmerding III Hockey Rink is packed. Ice hockey is one of few pro-caliber boarding school sports, so the crowd is big and screaming, numbers greasepainted on faces. College coaches and NHL scouts hide in the stands with notepads and cell phones.

But Delia, Greg, Gabriel, and Chase are united in more than just team spirit. They keep looking at one another, grinning madly, wondering what will happen when the Taft fans head back to their buses.

"Yay!" the Wellington fans scream as the final buzzer sounds and they're declared the winner.

People trickle out of the rink, entering the big, quiet night. Chase, Greg, Delia, and Gabriel scramble into a grove of birch nearby. They can almost hear the bugs. They fidget and whisper and giggle, waiting. Waiting. The cricket breeder from upstate showed up in his van earlier and Gabriel paid cash for the boxes. The guy made a king's ransom in one fell swoop. He usually supplies insects for feeding animals at pet stores and science labs and zoos. It took him days to amass this glistening, bony black splendor. He and Gabriel made the transaction like thugs in Morocco trading gold for opium. And now twenty thousand crickets hop and sing through the bus seats.

The overweight drivers are finishing their cigarettes in the dark end of the lot, while students meander up the steep bus steps. They disappear into the shadows of the vehicle. There's no sound. The crew looks at one another, wondering if the insects escaped already.

And then the screams. Bloodcurdling screeches and kids flying out the door, the drivers looking at each other and waddling as quickly as they can to their charges. The Wellington bunch high-five in the shadows, triumphant in this absurd errand, bonded.

The chirps sound as sweet as the screams of the students. And the locked windows of the climate-controlled buses mean there's only one exit for the critters. Taft might be here awhile. Greg throws his arm around Gabriel.

"Gabe, I love you, man. You're a genius."

Jamie drops Parker at the periphery of the school. They spent the evening watching *Dancing with the Stars* reruns, throwing things at the TV, eating Ritalin. Parker's euphoric, jumping out of her Saturday-night skin. As she slides out of the truck's interior, Jamie reaches across to her. He presses pills into her palm, the way an old lady who lives on Parker's hometown street used to press chocolate mints into her hand when she visited.

"Little present from the cookie jar," he says. "They'll help you come down."

"Thank you."

"Hope you don't think it rather creepy, me givin' these to you. I happen to think it creepy when people *hoard* their stash, you know what I mean?" he asks laughingly. "Just don't want you thinkin' I'm some sorta pusher."

"Please," Parker says, jacked up and friendly. "I would never think that about you, Jamie."

She stands in snowy woods, waving to his dark silhouette as he drives away. Above her, in a maple, an owl watches.

In Westport, a bride is helped into a glossy black Rolls-Royce and sent to her future. She sips champagne in the car, laughing with her new husband and pretending in the dark that she does not long for her childhood as it fades down the driveway. The estate collapses into a dollhouse, so small that in the future she'll be able to reach nothing but her hand inside.

On the highway, buses caravan in the moonlight, full of cowering kids; black insects crawl the metal walls, feeling with antennae for a way out.

At Wellington, Noah walks Laine to her dorm. She's wearing a fur stole inherited from her grandmother, and when they get to the stone stoop, she smiles apologetically, and slips out of reach like a figure in a dream. Climbing the stairs, she takes one shoe off and then the other, because her feet hurt. She feels stupid for running away. Why should a kiss be so frightening?

Laine is surprised to realize she's crying. She must be tired, or that one flute of champagne did it to her, or the long drive.

9

ood morning, Monday.

Noah's grumpy. He keeps deconstructing the wedding. He even asked one of his sisters what she thought of Laine, and she smiled and told Noah that Laine likes him. But then in the hired car, Laine went to sleep. Or pretended. She seemed repulsed by his closeness, pressing herself into the pleather interior.

And in a way Noah feels like he did something wrong, too, by taking Laine. The skirmish he and Chase had bothers Noah. Chase is his brother here. They've been friends since day one.

He walks down the hall of Cell Block D to the bathroom, shaves without paying attention, and nicks himself.

"Well, goddamn it," he says, pressing toilet paper to the cut.

Pebbled privacy windows are frosted with steam. Greg lumbers out of the shower, a royal-blue towel tucked around his waist, flip-flops on to keep from getting athlete's foot from the tiles.

"Yo, put Neosporin on that. Swear it stops the bleeding real fast," he counsels Noah. "I got some, if you need."

"Cool," Noah says, following Greg back to their room.

The hall is stirring. Kanye West bumps behind a door; blue computer light shines from Mark and Andrew's room; Jessie walks out in his tweed coat and West Point pom-pom hat. Greg tosses Noah the tube from his dresser.

"Thanks."

"Why you up anyway? Thought you had a sleep-in."

"I'm studying with Laine."

"With Mrs. Chase Dobbs?" Greg says.

"She doesn't belong to him."

"I know. Tell him that."

"What do *you* think?" Noah asks.

Greg rolls Old Spice under his arms. "He'll get pissed if you go near that, but he has no rights. He liked her for all the wrong reasons. You like her for the right reasons."

"Seriously?"

"*I* think so. Don't be afraid, man. You two seem like you'd be good together."

Noah decides to wear a new shirt. He unfolds it from its tissue, taking out pins. Why does he let Chase make him feel bad? Who's Chase? Noah frowns into the antique mirror, mouthing his side of this imaginary debate. What makes him especially nuts is that he knows Chase and Laine fooled around because Chase used to talk to Noah about it. Then it made Noah curious, and impatient for a girlfriend of his own. Now it makes him insane. It's like she's still with Chase, her face forever tilted to his, available, beautiful, her eyes half closed. The image is plastered in his head like posters glued all over Manhattan. Every corner he turns, there they are, advertising some love he'll never get.

He keeps going over the moral ground as he walks to the library. He's on fire when he arrives, more certain of his position. He pulls off his pom-pom hat when he enters the warm building.

"Oh God, I'm lost already," Laine says when he walks up.

"We'll fix that," he says.

He and Laine spend an hour in a nook. Their leather armchairs back up against an arched window of snowscape. She's wearing a sea-green sweater, wool skirt, and riding boots. Her blond hair is pulled off her face. He can't help thinking that she looks like an old-school movie star.

"What's 'scarcity' again?" she asks, as they go through terms for the quiz.

"It's, uh"—he underlines notes with his finger—"the

tension between limited resources and what some economists think of as the endless needs and wants of human beings. It's one of the basics of the science."

"The 'dismal science,'" she says.

"But I don't think it is, do you? I got *no* shame when it comes to admitting I don't want to be poor."

"Yeah, I know what you mean," she says slowly, as money is never mentioned inside these walls.

"Seriously. My family went to Verbier, in the Swiss Alps, for Christmas. To this chalet of a family we know. Ed Stetterson? Heard of him? Runs a hedge fund called Dover." Here Noah can't help the admiration from creeping into his voice; he collects finance-world players like baseball cards. "You should have seen this place."

"Over the top?" Laine asks.

"Dude. It was just beautiful, like, not a McMansion. Just classy. A cedar sauna. These reading areas where you sit and look at the mountains, under a reading lamp with a fur blanket and shit. A pool where the walls and the basin are all gray quartz. It was beyond."

"That sounds amazing."

Noah doesn't mention Ed's wife, Kate. She's not beautiful in a cover-of-*Maxim* way. Kate's delicate, but has a strong voice, as confident as any man in the room, or more so. She made everyone feel at home. The house was rich with treasure: dark chocolate from Brussels, Jo Malone soap, Turkish towels. She runs a luxurious ship. Ed's lucky.

And on Wall Street, Noah's father confided, Ed's pursuit and winning of Kate is legendary.

She reminds Noah of Laine.

"It *was* amazing," he answers. "And it really made me think about what I want in my future, you know? It's not just a house. Or a trip. I want to send my kids to whatever school they want, and I want them to travel." Noah sounds self-important talking about this future family. "I want them to be safe. Money is safety in this world, you know?"

Laine nods. There's a glow in each one's face, like cats who have decided to hunt together. Two capitalists on a snowy day in Connecticut.

"I totally know," she says.

"We should hang out more. We make a good team," Noah jokes, not sure where he got the balls to say this.

"Yeah, why not?" she says, chewing on her pen.

And Noah knows he scored a point here, moved them forward a notch. How did that happen? He was aggressive, but polite. One part manners, one part strength. Maybe he's finally cooking up his own formula.

Mr. Joyner stands in the admissions den, talking to Upperforms about college applications and the SATs. Tension hangs in the air like body odor.

"The goal is for each of you to find your way to that special place where you belong," he says warmly.

The school is being very careful this year about articulating pressure regarding college applications. It doesn't mean they're being gentle. They're just being vague. Each elite prep school has end-of-the-day statistics on where its students get accepted. It's like a business earnings report for a company, and the most important marketing tool for attracting new students (or attracting the parents who will pay the tuition).

Every boarding school wants to be a Harvard factory. Way back when, these halls teemed with the cream of society, schoolboys who stood to inherit the nation. Now that the system is more merit based, the descendants of robber barons have to beat out math prodigies from Korea for that hallowed "yes" from Yale. The family name doesn't have as many teeth as it once did.

"You can actually make studying for the SATs fun. I swear to you, I wouldn't lie. Make some flashcards. Sit down with your friends. Get into it."

No matter how Mr. Joyner puts it, this is a bloody endeavor. Parker, sitting in the back, blows imaginary spitballs of death at him. He's full of it. Parker looks at an antique map of Connecticut on the wall, and thinks about how they just got here, and now they're being prodded and hustled to the next place, the next dream, the next achievement. Like cows fattened, then sent to the slaughterhouse. *God, leave me alone.*

It doesn't help that her mom called this morning, and let slip that a grant didn't come through, and her dad's speaking engagement at the state university was called off. Her mother's information made Parker newly and freshly anxious about how much the Coles dish out on top of loans for Parker to be here.

Parker was already in a funk because she took Lisabet's study drugs last night to finish a physics paper, and then took Jamie's Xanax to sleep. She's still wading through chemical sleepiness. The girls have a plethora of uppers on Parker's floor, and they all share. It's getting Parker through the work, but killing her sleeping patterns.

"Thank you all; you guys are bright stars! Come to me with any questions at all, and we're going to take these next great steps together!" Mr. Joyner says.

Parker breaks from the herd. The halls smell like wet marble, from snow tramped on boots. The smell will always remind her of this time in her life. Sam and Mercer are talking so everyone can hear; they want the world to know they're going to Aspen together for spring break, *blah blah*. *SHUT UP,* Parker thinks. She drills their small brains with an ultraviolet laser beam of scorn.

She wears her fur hat inside, as a shield from the ignorance drifting like pollen through these corridors. The gold dust of overprivilege.

How did I get so angry? She's never felt the way she feels this week. Sometimes she does feel like a star, literally on top of the world, emitting centuries of light, untouchable. And then later she wants to *explode* like a star, spray-painting the sky with glitter, and turning into a black hole.

By the time she gets to the drama studio, she's dragging. When the bell rings, Mrs. Jenkins starts vocal warm-ups.

"The sixth sick sheik's sixth sheep's sick," they say in unison. "The sixth sick sheik's sixth sheep's sick."

They break into groups to read parts. Parker and Jorgen stand in a corner, where two mirrors meet. He's got chapped lips, and ink stains on his white cuffs. But she doesn't hate him. Today, with the way she feels, that's something.

"'Give me my Romeo; and, when he shall die,/ Take him and cut him out in little stars,'" she starts.

Cut him into stars. Jorgen isn't afraid to watch her face as she says these dangerous things. There's something about Jorgen that makes him different from every other guy she knows. He's fearless.

"'Cut him out in little stars,'" she continues. "'And he will make the face of heaven so fine/ That all the world will be in love with night,/ And pay no worship to the garish sun.'"

In love with night.

In this room, doubly reflected, motorcycle boots grounded on hardwood, she's free from herself. She's not Parker.

She's Juliet.

10

And here it comes, the notorious day. The box on the calendar crossed with blood. Valentine's Day. *Yay*.

There's the rose tradition, where for a dollar you have a rose placed in someone's mailbox with a note. The boxes fill with scrolls and flowers, sexual daydreams in Hallmark style. Chase tries not to remember last year. Schuyler in the dark, her presence like a toxic gas that made him delirious with lust, and also sick. Her ghostly hand afterward, running a wand of lip gloss over her mouth. The shame that almost broke his back, bending his spine as if he were a toy. He lies in bed, his alarm on snooze, his sheets pulled from the mattress in restless sleep. *I gotta get up*.

The way he figures, he might as well confront the holiday. See what the guys are doing. Get into something.

In the loo, Gerry and Jim Kwan are flossing and using astringent on their oily skin. Gerry is lisping about some RPG, how to get the jackpot dinosaur from under the green boulder.

"Boys," Chase warns, spitting toothpaste. "Not now. Too much excitement in the morning gives you indigestion."

Jim tries a laugh, but isn't sure. Both are shy around Chase. They admire and dislike him. Gerry, in a red tie with white stripes (Chase prays to *God* it's not a nod to V-Day), asks who Chase is taking to the dance tonight.

Chase thinks of making a joke. "My left hand." Or "Rita Lynn." Or "Mary Jane." But these guys wouldn't get it, or if they did, it would be tomorrow. So he's cryptic, and says: "The lucky winner."

The nerds look at each other, agree not to pursue.

"What about y'all?" Chase holsters his brush.

"I'm taking Casey Markon," Jim says.

"Leslie Hannigan; she's a Prep," Gerry says.

They sound like they're answering a teacher's question about homework. But that doesn't help Chase when he's walking down the white path and doing the math. They each have someone, and he has no one.

He eats an English muffin with raspberry jam in the dining hall, slurps coffee, and hits film class. Once again, it's snowing. Dr. P makes a grid on the board. The bulky man turns around. "Bergman," his voice booms, jump-starting discussion.

Parker doodles. The way she just looked at Chase—Chase who she hung out with last week, who she finally talks to, Chase who wants to make amends—she could have killed a grown man.

Parker's drawing candy hearts. Inside each one she writes in ballpoint script: *I hate you.* She's remembering last year too. How she believed—it's so amazing now that she could be this stupid—Chase Dobbs would ask her to the dance. And that she would borrow Nikki's halter dress, throw on the vintage dusty-rose heels, and somehow masquerade through the night as someone Chase could love.

And then he went with the blond, anorexic, coke-fiend of a proctor who had written on Parker's arm that she was ugly.

When oh when will these memories subside, and old hurts and angers be extinguished? *Because I'm ready,* Parker thinks. She thought she'd finished being vengeful. *Guess not.* When the bell rings, she hustles out before making eye contact again. She longs to open the cage and release all the people she begrudges, set them free like zoo animals, send them into the wild. She pictures Chase as a zebra, and that makes her smile.

Chase finally hunts down Noah and Greg in their room. "Greggy, you bitch." He slumps on the bed in his camel-hair coat. "I bet you got a date tonight."

"Yup," Greg says, ironing his shirt. "How'd you guess?"

Chase shakes his head, as though pitying his friend and the ball and chain he's dragging to the pink-cupcake-and-Mountain-Dew party. "Leaving me and Noah here to sadly sip our Maker's Mark and crush some Xanax for dessert. Who knows, with all the losers in my dorm I may just be able to snake a Prep on her way home."

The quick look between Noah and Greg says it all. They don't even smile at Chase's daily self-pity segment. It's Noah who spells it out.

"Um," Noah says, scratching his blue-black curls. "Yeah, about that. I'm actually going with Laine."

Chase answers too fast. "Of course you are." And he knows he just showed his cards. Time to head back to the lockup and shuffle his solitaire deck. Watch cartoons from New Zealand on YouTube. Download clips of amateur porn.

Noah is saying more, but Chase isn't listening. *SHUT UP.*

Delia and Laine make unlikely partners in crime, but Nikki's in Manhattan with Seth, eating Domino's delivered to his dank room and throwing chocolates from a red box at each other and saying sweet nothings and doing some heavy petting. Laine's in Delia's room, perched on the bed in a canary-yellow Ungaro dress with gray pearls around her neck. On the wall is a poster of Jack Johnson with a guitar.

"I'm glad Noah stepped up," Delia says, running Mitchum under one arm. "I was like, *yeah*, sugar. *Ask the girl.*"

Laine marvels at the slow Cali slide of Delia's sentences. She's never in a hurry. But she looks funny; she belongs in Reefs and Hawaiian shorts, white bangles against sun-gold skin. Not a tight black dress and gunked-up eyeliner, her thick, wavy hair slicked against her head into a ponytail. She has Mickey Mouse ears. She looks scared.

"It's so funny, because Noah's always been there, but I never thought we would, you know, be like this," Laine says, attempting an even voice although she's nervous as a rabbit about tonight.

"That's how it goes," Delia says, fussing with growing frustration in the mirror.

"I guess."

"What the hell!" she finally says. She implores Laine: "What's wrong with all this?"

Laine stands up. Delia makes her skittish; well, most girls do. She indicates Delia's hair. "Why don't you take it down? It looks pretty down," Laine says, adding the last part because she thinks it's what someone like Nikki would say.

"You think?" Delia says, her shoulders flexing as she untwists the band and shakes out her mane.

Laine appraises. "Maybe take off some eye makeup, do a

smoky thing. That would be nice."

They go through jewelry. Delia doesn't have anything nice, not like stuff Laine has been handed down: the emerald ring, the baby pearls from her great-grandmother, the signet ring. Delia has junk from the mall, Gwen Stefani–inspired gold chains, punk baubles. Laine pulls out cheap aquamarine earrings—plastic, but kind of beautiful.

Laine smiles. "Yeah, Noah's cool. He's grown up in a sense."

"What do you mean?"

"He was just a lackey to Chase for a while. Never really had his own persona, you know? I was sort of similar when I got here." Laine can't believe how forthright she's being, or how good it feels.

Delia puts an arm around her. "Sometimes being the coolest kid at fifteen doesn't always end up well."

They laugh. They both have baggage and it's not a secret. They laugh about being screwed up, and it's exhilarating. The black limousine pulls up in the white snow. It's not new; the fins have a 1970's attitude, and the car's luster is hard-won.

The girls look out the window as the guys step out of the vehicle, awkwardly, slipping on ice, flowers in hands. The moon's reflection pools on the car's roof like milk. Laine likes Delia. They'll be decent co-dates—like wives who know no one else in a new suburban neighborhood.

As the girls step delicately into the night, Chase is alone, staring out his window and wishing he had a BB gun to take off the pom-poms on the hats of the Summer loser squad carrying orchids—wilting from the cold, catching snowflakes on magenta-speckled petals—to pick up their Prep dates. He watches them leave his dorm, these Upper-forms and seniors who never went to the dance and are finally old enough to finagle a Prep who won't go with the superloser in her own class but will go with an older one.

His in-room phone rings. He lets it ring. He aims the phantom rifle at it and pulls the trigger. On the seventh ring he answers.

"Yo," he says.

"Hey," she says, in this snide, I-don't-know-why-the-hell-I'm-calling-you voice.

"Parker Cole," he drawls. "Did you call to wish me a happy Valentine's Day?"

"Ha!" she says. "You're funny."

"*I* know, you called to tell me you hate me," he says, having more weird fun than he's had all day.

"I called to tell you that Jamie's picking me up behind the tennis courts in twenty, if you want to tag along."

And she hangs up.

He ponders it for approximately thirty seconds.

He watches the black angel of moon shadow on the snow as he walks, and stares at the limo that slushes past, unaware his buddies are inside. Going to Jamie's is opening Pandora's box. But it's better than sticking around the dorm and counting sheep. He pulls his Remington hat low, squeezes the bill. His coat hangs unbuttoned, and his hands are bare, his suede bucks scuffed and unlaced. He's open, inviting whatever comes next to come to him.

Parker's open too, in a sense. She doesn't know why she called, why she invited him. It's like dangling raw steak against the cage of a dog, out of his teeth's reach. Why do people do such things? Even Moses bares his fangs and wags his tail at the same time, confused by how affectionate Parker is when she kneels in the hall to kiss him good-bye.

11

From the limousine, Gabe sees Chase walking, but doesn't lower the tinted window. He turns in the leather seat and smiles at Seiko. She's wearing a kajillion-dollar dress, and carrying a Louis Vuitton clutch. Street lamps slide over her face, flicker in her black eyes. He and Seiko are from different continents but the same world. She's at home in a chauffeured car. She holds up her glamorous head as they drive through the Podunk countryside.

The driver is Wayne, who also works in the dining hall; this town is so small it's like a play with a few cast members who take on multiple parts. Wayne smiled when the crew got in and were shocked to see him. He's wearing a cheap suit and a gold bracelet, and has razor burn on his pale neck.

"Don't worry, you guys," he said to them, grinning and snapping his gum. "I'm working for the car service right now, you know what I'm saying? Not for the school."

So Greg and Delia covertly sip Hennessy. They pass it to Gabe, who takes a taste, but Seiko waves it away with a slender hand. And Laine looks to Noah. She doesn't want cognac on her breath; she already got booted once. She knows how it feels to be driven through the gates, to look over your shoulder and see the red light blinking like a heart, and believe this would be the last passage.

"I'm good," Noah says, waving it away, after catching fear in Laine's eyes. *Screw it,* he thinks. *I can behave if it's worth it.*

Wayne opens their doors, and everyone suppresses smiles as they step into the parking lot of the Dakota Range Steakhouse; it seems weird for the guy who ladles them some soupy macaroni to be playing chauffeur.

"Bon appetito," Wayne says.

Inside, the maître d' looks up their reservation, and takes their coats. In the center of the white-clothed tables are scarlet begonias and orchids. The room is wallpapered in emerald, and there's a hush of luxury, a fragrance of prime rib and cabernet and crème brûlée, of women's perfume and men's shaving cream, and of flowers. The group is seated, and they unfold napkins and take the menus handed to them.

"I'm starving," Greg says, eyes running down the page.

"Me too," Delia says, her fingers curling one of her locks as she leans over to read Greg's menu, leaving her own closed.

"I wonder what Wayne's doing now," Noah says with a wry smile.

"Bringing his baby mama some McDonald's," Greg quips. "And supermarket daisies."

"I like Wayne," Delia says. "I like how he was playing soft rock for us. Very romantic."

The table laughs.

"Yeah, I just love Celine Dion," Laine ventures, to more laughter.

"It's the thought that counts," Seiko purrs, not quite meaning it but with nice intentions.

And at this, Noah relaxes. Because he made it. He's here. Three couples, six people who like one another. Six upstanding human beings who are going to order some red meat and drink their Coca-Colas like obedient citizens and share chocolate mousse. He's never been part of something like this. He's always been the third wheel, or fifth wheel, or seventh wheel. Laine is crazy beautiful. The banana-yellow silk. Those pearls. He's lucky. They're all lucky winners. And even if Noah and Laine are still nothing but friends, he can tell she's thinking of more. She looks at him longer; she sits closer.

Meanwhile, Chase and Parker are chauffeured by someone else. Jamie picks them up, the Ark blaring in strange and atonal glory.

"What's up, you li'l bloody valentines?" he asks with a devious grin as he drives an uneven line on the snowy road. He holds up one of his fingerless-gloved hands to the back-seat for Chase to slap, which Chase does, with chagrin.

"Can we pretend it's Christmas or something?" Parker asks, writing *Parker* in the fog she blew onto her window. "Like, anything but Valentine's Day."

"Yeah, let's make it my birthday," Jamie says in that lazy British accent.

"Happy birthday, brother," Chase says from where he lounges in the back.

Everything's copacetic, but deep in his gut Chase feels belligerent. Jamie's the host with the most, and goddamn, he's Chase's ticket from dormitory hell tonight. But something makes Chase clench his fists. *Something about this guy just makes me want to asphyxiate him with his suspenders.*

At the house, they see George's vintage pewter Bugatti, its windows tinged yellow from years of cigar smoke. All the curtains of the house are drawn so they can't see inside, but through the cracks shine beads of chandelier and candle-light. Sunk into the snow on the stoop are bottles of Veuve Clicquot. Jamie yanks the E-brake. He hops out, swaggers in skinny jeans to the bottles, vulnerable as bowling pins, and snags two.

He gets back into the jeep and rolls down to the pool house. "They stick those out there to get cold, yeah? We're just going to have to exact what they call a luxury tax on 'em."

They stamp up the stairs to find Sophie and her friend Ray (who's a girl) dancing like they're on pogo sticks to Le Tigre. Ray must be a model too, as her clavicle is chiseled microscopically, and she wears yellow eye shadow. Her zebra slip is 1986 suburban newlywed, and her feet are dirty from dancing. Sophie looks the same as last time; Chase wonders if she bathes or changes.

"What up!" Ray calls out over the music.

"Hey, guys," Sophie says, grinding her jaw.

Jamie mimics them by jumping up and down to the beat for a minute, holding the bottles to his sides. Then he stops abruptly and calmly walks to the counter, unwraps the foil from one neck, and pops it. Suds flood and everyone squeals. Jamie beckons Parker; he tips her face back and lets the stuff fill her mouth.

Chase lounges on a chair, reading spines of books on Jamie's shelf. Vintage copies of *Fear and Loathing in Las Vegas* and *Delta of Venus*. A few pornographic comic books. And two university press books on making bombs at home. *This guy Jamie, what a charmer.*

When the song's over, the model twins flop on the bed, sweating. Parker sees blue dust ringing Ray's nostril. She tries not to stare, but Ray touches her finger to her nose.

"Am I dirty?" Ray asks.

"Not really," Parker says, not knowing the etiquette.

"Yes, I *am*," Ray responds, looking at the robin's egg blue on the tip of her pinkie.

"You want a line?" Sophie asks.

"Um . . ." Parker tries to make a benevolent face out of her grimace.

"Of what?" Chase asks, slouching with his arms crossed behind his honey-streaked head.

"Adderall," Ray says, bringing a CD case from under the coffee table, where five chunky lines of powder sit, the antivenom to Valentine's Day.

"Bring it on," Chase says, sitting up.

Parker makes an inscrutable face at Chase—not mean, not kind, but she looks him in the eye. "I'll have one too," she concedes.

"Have you ever snorted anything, Park?" Chase asks.

"No." She shrugs. "But it can't be that hard if you losers can do it."

And *bang*, they're out of the gate.

While the band of freaks sniffs the blue in a pool house in town, the steakhouse gang is driving in the black Lincoln limousine to the dance at the gym. Gabriel burps and tries to keep it in his fist, but it doesn't work and Seiko laughs at him, looking like a girl for the first time tonight instead of a refined twenty-something-year-old. Delia rests her sleepy and satisfied face on Greg's pin-striped lapel as Greg uses a toothpick. Laine and Noah sit close, feel the heat of each other's leg.

"You got to hand it to the party planners. This is a dynamite setup," Gabriel says sarcastically as they enter the gym to red crepe streamers draped over trophy cases.

"Absolute mayhem," Noah quips in a Locust Valley Lockjaw accent, and only then realizes that somehow he and Laine are holding hands. He peeks at her and she seems happy.

The deejay is a forty-something local guy with a bald spot and too many earrings. He's spinning the brutal classics: from Cher to Kelly Clarkson to Vanilla Ice and back again. The gym is spangled by the disco ball, and there are plenty of dark corners. The punch bowl shines on the dessert table.

At first Noah and Laine stand at the periphery and make jokes, acting like they have no need for the dance floor. Noah rubs his jaw, knowing he has to get them off the sidelines. They look like scaredy-cats. He's watched the maestros, the senior guys who have *perfected* irony, who come to these things looking good, but with a wig or a purple top hat or a silver cigarette case of joints. And to watch them dance you'd think they were serious, but they're doing a wink-wink thing that girls love. The guys who don't participate at all come off concerned about appearances.

The deejay throws on Christina Aguilera's "Beautiful" and Noah tracks his buddies from the corner of his eye. Gabe is leading Seiko into the mob. Greg takes Delia out there, throwing away their paper plates, wet with strawberry ice cream. Noah's heart thuds like a brick dropped from a high window onto dirt.

"Shall we? Can't be left behind, can we?" he says.

She shrugs, and they enter the fray. At first they playact, pretending to be serious ballroom dancers, mimicking the fandango, laughing out of anxiety. But somehow they slow down, press together, and dance. Or sway. There's heat between their bodies, where yellow silk meets black gabardine. Noah is not on this earth anymore. He's in the red zone.

Parker's in the blue zone. She got a lesson from the group on rolling her dollar bill and snorting the powder. It burned so badly she clutched her face and yelped, which made everyone fall off their seats, laughing till they were breathless.

But she can feel it move, stinging her blood vessels, waking her up—blue snow in her mind.

Everyone's talking fast; there's euphoria in telling stories. Parker wants to open the cupboards of her past and show everyone what's inside. Ray has the tattoo of a seahorse on her inner wrist and tells Parker a long story about some guy named Jackson who was bipolar and a Taco Bell in Florida and a plane crash where everyone turned out to be okay. Parker listens with every fiber of her being, even clutching Ray's hand at the hard parts for moral support, but after the tale is told, Parker would be hard-pressed to recall it, or say what it had to do with a seahorse tattoo.

"I *love* your teeth," Sophie tells Chase, and she's dead serious.

"Thank you," Chase says, and so is he.

Everyone does another line. Then another, for good luck.

"I'm a monkey, you fools," Jamie says with delight as he jumps over the back of the couch. He drains the Veuve Clicquot and holds it to the light. "We're going to play spin the bottle."

Two miles away, Noah is a millimeter from kissing Laine, from cupping her chin and putting his mouth to hers, when Christina Aguilera morphs into Eminem, and couples pull apart, wiping their eyes as if just waking. Noah's cold.

He and Laine loiter at the cookies. She takes a pink iced heart and nibbles on it. All night she's been evaluating Noah. He reminds her of JFK Jr. And he's behaving. He doesn't push or pull her; he's not dangerous like

Chase. Chase was too much. He wanted things too badly. He took what he wanted, or tried. Noah stands now, freckles of light crossing his face, his Yves Saint Laurent tie unstained. His hands in his own pockets.

In the pool house, Sophie kisses Ray, a short peck, and everyone claps. Jamie kisses Sophie, a shorter peck. Then Chase spins the champagne bottle and lands on Jamie.

"Oooooh," the girls all say.

Jamie gives Chase a daredevil look. "You wanker, you're afraid."

"Afraid?" Chase asks, burning from pills and fear. "Not really."

"You think I want to kiss your ugly face, then?" Jamie asks with decadent ridicule in his tone. He holds out his hand. "Try this."

Chase actually blushes. To do it would mean submitting to this ego. Not to do it would make Chase look prudish, scared. He bends down and does the first thing instincts lead him to do: He bites Jamie's fingers.

"Holy bloody Christ!" Jamie shouts, waving his hand in the air, and then clutching it. "You piece of shite, Chase! Snort my pills, drink my beers, and bite my fucking hand, mate!"

Chase stares at Jamie, surprised himself at what he just did, and when Jamie gets quiet and just looks at him, Chase feels the hair on his neck stand up in expectation of a wallop across the mouth.

"You're fucking funny," Jamie whispers then, and everyone starts laughing, the tension dispelled—for a moment. It's Jamie's turn, and he gets Parker.

"You aimed it that way!" Sophie cries out.

Jamie gives her an evil grin, and leans to Parker, who looks down, bashful. He kisses her quickly, but tenderly. Chase sees fire. Parker licks her lips nervously, and puts her hand to her cheek.

"Whoa," she says. The veins in her neck are visibly pulsing, from drama and drugs. "Uh, I guess it's my turn."

And as it happened in a million rainy-day fantasies of hers, the bottle spins and spins and spins and spins, and slowly stops in Chase's direction. They smile sadly, as they both know this kiss is too late. Chase kneels, holds her hair away from her beautiful mouth, and pauses to look at her before he kisses her. Once they start, though, they can't stop. It's a slow pleasure, impossible to give up. Even with her heart beating quadruple-time, the world stands still.

Suddenly Chase gets a blow to the shoulder, which separates him from Parker. It was Jamie, who betrays for one second a look of hatred. Before Chase can process what happened, he pushes Jamie back, using a flat hand to Jamie's chest, but hitting him harder than he means to. Jamie falls onto the floor, then releases his muscles and lies back as if sleeping. Everyone looks at one another with concern until Jamie starts cackling like a hyena.

Noah and Laine are standing on an upper floor of the gym, having wandered there with nothing else to do. They stand, reflected in the glass wall, looking over swimming lanes of the Olympic pool below. The ghost of chlorine seeps through the pane. They're having an inane pre-kiss conversation, so caught up in what's about to happen they're making first-grade sentences.

"I like swimming," Noah says, jingling an empty money clip in his pocket. "Do you?"

"Yeah, I really do," Laine says, fingering the pearls around her neck.

"I mean, I don't really love doing laps," Noah says.

"Yeah, me neither. Except sometimes I do like it."

With each moronic statement, they drift closer. Their voices get lower, sentences shorter. But—

"What's up, luv-*ahs*," Greg says, his jacket over his shoulder, Delia's hand in his, both striding with post-sex vigor and looseness. "Wayne, the man behind the wheel, requests our presence. Time to hit it."

Jamie is showing Parker how to wash the coating off an OxyContin so she can feel it sooner.

"What *is* OxyContin?" she asks, running her hand along the Provençal tiles in the bathroom. Her pupils are like cartoon stars.

Jamie laughs. "Oh, lassie. You're like the last little girl on earth to know, aren't you? Where you been hidin', luv?"

Everyone takes a pill to come down. It's not long after that that Parker's mouth droops and her eyelids hang. She pukes in the middle of the room, as if trying to hit the center. *Bull's-eye. You got it, kid.*

Noah's racking his brain, because Seiko and Laine live in the same dorm, so even though Wayne will drop off Delia first, he and Gabriel will both have to kiss their dates at the same time outside. He wonders if Laine will go for it. He has a notion this is going to be a kissless V-Day, and that is going to hurt. It will hurt deeply. It will hurt all night long and into tomorrow. Next week, it's still going to hurt.

Wayne herds them into the limo, and students leaving the dance either glare or smile. Everyone's moving slowly, dreading being contained in their dorms. It's twenty minutes to Check In. Laine climbs in before Noah, and he gets to see a stretch of perfect leg under the yellow silk. It's like a piece of candy.

* * *

Ray stays away from the mess. Sophie hands wetted paper towels without getting too close. Chase holds Parker's hair back, looking at his watch. Jamie's got the bucket.

"Shit," Chase says. "We got, like, twenty minutes."

"What's the big deal?" Jamie asks.

Chase feels his face heat up instantly, and even though his mind and tongue are slowed and thickened with Oxy, he curses Jamie out. "What's the big *deal*? It's your god-damn fault, and I am *not* getting Parker kicked out and I am *not* getting my ass booted because you gave her too much fucking stuff."

"She's a big girl," Jamie says, but he looks pale and strange, like a little boy. No megawatt smile. When he meets Chase's eyes, Chase can see he's worried and sorry.

"This is crazy," Chase says, and looks away. "You need to figure this out."

"Easy, Chase," Jamie says, flipping back into aggression. "Don't come to my house, party with us, and start telling *us* what to do. This is not our bloody problem. You and the lady should have thought of this."

Chase is too angry to respond.

Parker wipes her mouth a last time and sits on her heels. "We gotta go," she slurs, her eyes misty.

"I know," Chase agrees darkly.

They look at each other.

129

"I'll drop you at the tennis courts," Jamie says.

Chase and Parker search each other's face. Finally Chase says, "Yeah. Let's do that." Even though Jamie shouldn't be driving.

The models have flipped on *Late Night*, and are falsely gracious as Chase, Parker, and Jamie leave. The girls wave like pageant winners, making it obvious they abhor rookies. The three of them walk through knee-high snow; flakes have been falling for hours. Chase supports Parker, and fears there's no way in hell he can get her into the dorm without a scandal. And this means expulsion.

Chase sits in the back with Parker. They swerve and slip on the road, and Jamie plays no music and looks back with screwed-up, hollow eyes to see how she is. She hangs her head into the wind, and Chase thinks she might be crying—not sobbing, just letting tears fall from the corners of her eyes into the snow.

When they get out, Jamie grabs Chase's shoulder. "Listen."

"It's cool," Chase says, and tries to smile. "Better get out of here; you're just going to bring attention."

As Jamie drives away, they limp a short way through the birch grove behind the courts. The school is a blaze of windows a quarter mile up the hill. Chase smells Parker's violet perfume; her skin is shiny with sweat even though it's cold out. Her black leather motorcycle jacket hangs open.

Suddenly she crumples. She sits cross-legged in the snow, head hanging.

"Park," Chase says, squatting, holding her face.

"No, no, no," she wails. "I can't walk."

"Park," Chase says desperately, looking at his watch. "Babe, you gotta walk."

The snow is wetting her jeans. Her hair makes a curtain to her face. Suddenly she takes hold of Chase's forearms and pulls him down into her, so that he's holding her. And she cries. She's fucked up.

He kisses her neck, and he feels sick himself. Because he knows now, for certain and forever, that he loves this girl. That this is the one. And he also knows that even if she stood up right now, and they both ran to their dorms, they would still miss Check In. It's over.

The limousine, though, is on time. Wayne dropped off Delia, and is heading to Laine and Seiko's dorm. Then he'll drop the guys. Greg's eyes are closed, his head resting against the seat. Seiko's eating candy hearts out of her black clutch. No one's talking. Everyone's done. Wayne's still putting his touch on the night, playing Journey: "Don't Stop Believing." Noah is fighting bitterness, and hopefulness.

The long car is coming around the Blake trail when suddenly, out of nowhere, everything shatters. Literally. The windshield is cracked; the car is fishtailing. In slow motion, everyone will remember the crack, the glimmer, a thudding elsewhere, Seiko screaming, Wayne yelling to hold on and duck, a slow and bad slide, and then a strangely peaceful stop.

It feels like an hour before anyone can speak. Laine is certain Noah's dead, the way his neck is twisted. And Wayne's collar has blood on it.

"Oh my God," Seiko says. "Oh my God."

Gabriel brushes tiny blocks of glass from his jacket and starts to assess. "Seiko, are you okay? Laine?"

Each girl nods, touching her face and neck for blood.

Noah lifts his head before Gabriel gets to him, and Greg rubs his shoulder. They all look to Wayne, who hasn't moved. Noah reaches to the front and feels his throat. When he does, Wayne groans.

"Oh, man," the driver says without opening his eyes. "Who's hurt?"

"No one, Wayne," Noah says. "Are you?"

Wayne opens his eyes and looks back. A straight slash on his forehead is bleeding, but not terribly. "I'm okay."

They emerge from the vehicle in the snowbank. The girls, in dresses, look like hothouse flowers tossed into a winter night. Noah asks Wayne what happened, looking at the zigzag of tire tracks.

"That was a deer, man. Kicked the glass out."

Greg, who wandered back, confirms this. The hoof tracks have blood in them.

Laine is huddled next to Noah, shaking—almost bucking—with adrenaline, and cold. Wayne's on the radio to the dispatcher, his groggy voice getting more succinct as he relays details.

And there, with a red light streaking her dress and a bruise blossoming on her thigh, in the shadow of the dorm and in plain sight of half the school, Laine stands on her tiptoes and kisses Noah, long and hard.

When Parker can stand, it's well past Check In, at least ten minutes. They walk hand in hand, Parker apologizing over and over, her voice thick from crying. The moon casts branches onto their faces. Over and over, Chase tells her it's okay. But they both walk like they're doomed.

As they near Gray, Chase sees blue and red lights, and knows they're royally screwed. Parker stops walking. Chase shakes his head at her, indicating that they have no choice, and so they walk again. Her jeans are dark with wetness.

But it's an ambulance, actually two, and there's a lot of hustle. Chase, like a mother who can lift a car that's on top of her child, somehow corrals his strategic instincts for survival, and he runs, pulling Parker by the hand, to the basement door of her dorm. He opens it and pushes her inside.

"Go up to your room. Take a shower. Get in bed. Do *not* talk to anyone," he orders desperately in a hoarse whisper.

And he backs away, letting her close the door, and

hopefully she's going to do what he says. He walks around the long way, listening to voices. He hears Gabriel. *What??!*

Chase comes around the front, hands in pockets, hoping he can say he came out of his dorm to see what happened, and also hoping that whatever did actually happen is not as serious as it's looking. The siren lights twirl on the snow.

Noah's sitting on the back of one ambulance, and an EMS guy is looking him over. All of Gray is outside, some in party dresses and some in pajamas, and kids from other dorms mix in, too. All the floormasters are present, on cell phones, in emergency mode. Chase steps up to Noah. He's suddenly sober.

"What happened?"

Noah smiles wryly as the stethoscope disappears into his Prada shirt. "Deer. Limousine." He juts his chin down the hill.

Chase sees the wrecked limo, a black shark in white water.

"Holy shit. Who was in the car? Are you okay?"

Noah smiles again. "We're all going to live, man. Everything's good."

12

Every day, when Parker wakes up, she knows she loves Chase before she can even remember her own name or where she is. Ever since the Valentine's Day debacle last weekend, she's been floating through school, always looking for him, always finding him. He'll be in the dining hall, sipping chocolate milk, looking at gray winter framed in the antique window, and he'll turn as she approaches as if he has eyes in the back of his head, and he'll smile as he never smiled at her before.

"Hey, kid," he says softly.

"Hey," she says back.

He gets infused into everything. She thinks of him the whole time she's with her Rats, at play practice. At Wellington, Rats are art freaks. The kids who live underground in sculpture studios or music rooms. The boys with eye makeup and soprano voices. The girls with glasses, Manic Panic purple in their hair, and mismatched tube socks. Rats make assembly announcements that are complex inside jokes. Rats come to school in glow-in-the-dark clothes on free-dress days and eat beets and tofu cheese on whole-grain bagels for breakfast.

Jorgen is a prime Rat, a prodigy no one gets. In ten years he'll be Moby, fueled by high school trials, making millions. For now, he's Romeo so he can shirk the sports requirement.

"'Farewell, farewell! One kiss, and I'll descend.'"

Parker loves Jorgen's Swedish accent.

She recites: "'Art thou gone so? Love, lord, ay, husband, friend!/ I must hear from thee every day in the hour,/ For in a minute there are many days.'" Parker puts her script down. She inches toward Jorgen: "'O, by this count I shall be much in years/ Ere I again behold my Romeo!'"

Jorgen stops and stares at her. He seems nervous. "Are you already off script? Are we supposed to stand this close to each other?"

Parker backs away, scoffing. "What are you afraid of?"

Mrs. Jenkins saunters over, arms folded. "How you guys doing?"

Parker shrugs. "Good, I guess."

Mrs. Jenkins puts her arms around both Parker and

Jorgen. "You've got to think of someone you love when you deliver those lines, you guys."

Jorgen dips his eyes in John Briar's direction, and then blushes, looking at his own feet, and Parker finally gets it. *Duh.* Jorgen's gay. When he looks up again, Parker smiles at him. *It's all good,* she says with her eyes.

Talk about star-crossed! No matter how tolerant people claim to be these days, watching *Will & Grace* and voting for gay marriage or whatever, hate lingers in some imaginations. If Parker feels pressure to seek the conformists' paradise, how must he feel? He's starting from much farther outside of Eden. It can feel dangerous, wandering lost and cold.

That's why her childhood friend Blue is defiant. He's got the stature of a pit bull, even though he's gentle. If he lets down his guard among the wrong animals, he's dead meat. If these guys can be brave in who they love and how, then Parker might step up to the plate herself.

Boys' night. The high-performance demands of Upper-form spring drive students to drink. Or to do drugs. For Gabriel, Chase, and Greg, partying is as fun as study hall these days, something they do to show solidarity. It's work. It's medicine. It keeps the tattered end of winter in one piece. It holds them together one more night.

The first shot makes Chase gag. He used to love Jack Daniel's until two summers ago, when he went overboard in Folly Beach and had his stomach pumped. Gatorade cools the burning in his belly. The handle is passed to Greg, then to Gabriel.

"Ouch, that bites," Gabriel says.

The guys hide the bottle and reopen the door after round seven. A jar of peanut butter is passed; a spoonful covers liquor breath. Chase slouches on Gabriel's couch and chooses an old Pharcyde album on Gabriel's iPod dock.

"What time you all want to hit Main Building?" Greg asks, trying for a hint of indifference.

Neither Chase nor Gabriel responds.

"Where's Noah?" Chase asks.

Greg plays with the ties of his hoodie. "Playing Scrabble or something wholesome, probably, with those cornball hockey players."

Gabriel nods. "He's probably with Laine. You cool with it now, Chase? I've seen you walking around with Parker."

Chase rolls his eyes. "Crazy, huh? I know." Chase's answer is a nonanswer. Because he knows he shouldn't begrudge Noah, but at the same time he isn't ready to just let go of Laine. As for Parker, Chase is going with his gut, and not ready to be public.

"It's cool; we'll have a guys' night," Greg says.

"Let's head over," Chase agrees.

Chase sloshes over dirty snow in socks and Havaiana flip-flops. The snack bar line overflows into the hallway, but

Greg pushes through. The guys are getting that shine on, feeling like high rollers.

The trio orders Wank Burgers. It's good to fill their stomachs after the booze.

At the next table sits a certain clique of Preps in True Religion jeans and enough gold chains to make Mr. T jealous. Everyone calls them the Gossip Girls, due to their anorexia, money, and social climbing. The guys can't help but look; they're like a plate of cookies.

"Goddamnit. They keep getting younger, don't they," Greg muses, like a dirty old man.

Noah appears and sits down, his long face freshly shaved, his black Burberry coat buttoned up. "Howdy, people."

"Well, well. Where the hell have you been hiding?" Chase asks, trying to sound good-natured.

"I've been around. Just busy with hockey, and lax coming up. What's going on?"

"Just being our usual juvenile delinquent selves, kid. Nothin' much," Chase says, again trying for easy patter but sounding uptight.

"Yeah, I can smell," Noah says, getting a whiff of peanut butter and whiskey.

Chase turns red at this, unexpectedly. He blows his bangs out of his eyes. "Go ahead, dude. Off to the hockey table, big man. Don't want to keep you."

Noah looks at Chase. "I wasn't headed to the hockey

table, but if you need some space, I'll be glad to give it."

"Naw, man. Stay put," Greg says, trying to keep the crew together.

Chase looks down at his faded Levi's, pulls at the fringe around a hole in the denim. He should speak up but he doesn't.

"It's cool. I'm going to run," Noah says.

And even though Chase doesn't look up, he feels Noah looking at him as he stands and walks away. The buzz is dying.

Gabriel stands and stretches. "Shall we go grind Preps on the dance floor?" he asks sarcastically.

Greg licks his fingertip to pick up crumbs of bread off a plate. He shrugs.

Chase feels it too. He ruined the moment. He should apologize but doesn't know how. So much for guys' night. Greg wants to hang out with Delia, who's at the corner table with Nikki, and Gabriel wants to find Seiko. The problem for Chase is that Parker never comes to Saturday nights. He thought she *might* come tonight, to see him, but she's not here.

"Catch you later," Gabriel says, slapping Chase's hand as they part.

Greg salutes, saunters over to his girl.

I'm just going to do it, Chase thinks, his pride slippery with bourbon.

He heads to Gray, and waits on the steps until a pair of girls arrives at the stone building. Chase is shivering. He asks them to send Parker down.

She takes her time, and when she arrives in the arch of the front door, he can tell she was dozing. Her face is wrinkled and her eyes are foggy with sleep, sweet.

"Hi," she croaks, adjusting her sweatpants and Ramones T-shirt, rubbing her bare arms to stay warm.

"Hi," he says, wobbling.

"Whoo," she says, waving her hand at his breath.

"I know, I know," he mumbles.

"What are you doing here, Chase?"

He scratches his head. "I was wondering if you wanted to watch the film for class in the viewing room tomorrow?" He hiccups.

She laughs. "Sure. Ten o'clock?"

He hiccups again and smiles sloppily. The whiskey is catching up. "Yesh," he slurs.

She comes onto the cold stoop in her bare feet. She kisses his forehead and whispers: "Go to bed, baby. Be safe."

He backs away, dazed by the vision of long, tall Parker in the frame of the door, and by the stars above. Then he turns and runs, skidding over snowy ground, as fast as when he was a kid racing barefoot over South Carolina sand in the August sun.

* * *

He gets to the library late and rings the call button. Mrs. Vendemeer hobbles over. Cane in her left hand, pen in her right, and a grimace on her face.

"Mr. Dobbs, up early or just exiting detention?"

Chase smiles. "I'm here to watch a DVD for class. Do you know which room Parker Cole signed out?"

She removes her glasses and looks at him suspiciously. "Why?"

Chase is annoyed; Mrs. Vendemeer acts like he's going to shoot up in her viewing room. "Because we're watching it together," he says slowly for her to understand.

She primly reaches for the binder. "Room two-A."

Chase walks up deeply carpeted stairs. He taps on the door. His heart is going buck wild.

Parker cracks the door and rolls her eyes. "Remarkable. Late, as usual."

"But I'm here. And I bathed."

"Come *in*," she groans, and flops back on the couch.

An hour into the movie and Chase's head is lying on Parker's lap. She runs her fingers through his hair, sticks it straight up. He can feel her hand shaking but she tries to act calm.

"I was sad when you cut your hair last spring," Parker says quietly.

He rolls over and looks up at her. "Yeah, me too. But it

got me the right to go road-tripping, from my dad. Even though *someone* decided not to be home when I got to Canada."

"I guess it would be so crazy of me to expect a phone call first, to let me know you were coming."

"I thought you liked surprises."

She smiles. "I do."

He searches her face.

This makes her nervous, and she blushes. "Are you going to watch the movie?"

He shrugs. "I'm watching you."

She rolls her eyes. "You're a cheeseball."

Chase laughs.

She leans down and kisses him. "You really want to make out with me during *Psycho*?"

"I think it's fitting," he responds.

She laughs and slides below him. They giggle as they take each other's shirt off. It's a tangle of sleeves. Parker laughs when Chase stands up, erect in his boxer shorts, to check the lock.

"That's a nice look," she says, in a raspy, making-out voice.

Chase looks down and without a hint of embarrassment responds, "That just means he likes you." He falls back on top of her.

When the movie credits are rolling, and they're lying still in each other's arms, Chase gets an idea.

"Will you come visit me in Charleston over break?" he asks.

She melts, buries her face in his neck. He feels her nod.

13

After hockey practice, Noah and Laine find themselves at the center dining hall table. It's the training ground for a certain set. The next stop is a legendary fraternity or sorority, and if they're cool enough, a secret society like Skull and Bones at Yale. After that, the Tennis and Racquet Club, or the Colony Club. Safari clubs in Kenyas. Fishing clubs in Cabo San Lucas.

This is the I-banking team, the hedge funders, the philanthropists. The people whose names will appear in *The Wall Street Journal*, whose faces will show up on CNBC. This is the whale-belt and golf-glove-sunburn table. The kids who will run into one another yachting in Antigua, or chasing foxes in Virginia. It's a precious club.

And Trevor's the commodore.

"What else do we need to settle?" he asks.

The topic is May Day. The May Day Committee is an elite group of Upper-forms and seniors. Each year, a few new Upper-forms get tapped to join, and as much as everyone on the outside bitches about the snobby committee, May Day is the best party of the year. The volleyball tournament, the mudslide races, the raffle prizes, topped off by an up-and-coming band under the lights on Senior Lawn. The only thing missing is a keg in the parking lot.

Next to Laine is Caitlin French, a senior from Darien who invited Laine, and next to Noah is *his* sponsor, Trevor, the lacrosse captain. Even though Trevor hates him, in theory, for the Florida debacle, he invited Noah here for *something*.

"So, May Day is a month away, and we've got a ton of shit to do," Trevor says. With tousled blond hair, a J. Crew tweed blazer, and a Vineyard Vines tie, Trevor is cover material for the Wellington catalog. He also has the résumé: proctor in the freshman dorm, Disciplinary Committee elect, lacrosse captain, president of the school's Amnesty International group.

"We've got to lock down a band, design T-shirts and posters, do E-vites, pick a charity, and get raffle prizes." Trevor scans the table.

"Yeah, we've got a lot to do," Caitlin agrees.

"So, Noah, you want to help out with the raffle?" Trevor

looks at Noah, whose mouth is full of mashed potatoes. Before he can swallow, Trevor continues: "Isn't your mom on the board of the Boys and Girls Club in NYC?"

"Mm-huh." Noah makes an affirmative noise, almost choking on his potatoes.

"And isn't Tiki Barber their spokesman?"

Noah nods.

"So let's do this," Trevor says, which is his hallmark phrase. "How about one prize is a Giants game, sidelines with Tiki?" Trevor points a finger at Noah. "You work on that, okay?"

"Yeah, that would be so cool," Caitlin adds for good measure.

It would be cool but I have no idea if I can make that happen. Noah decides not to protest. "It could happen, I guess. I'll ask my mom."

"Fantastic." That's another of his favorite words. Trevor turns to Laine. "Laine, you'll help with the poster and T-shirt design, cool?"

"Sur-r-r-e?" Laine stumbles. "I'm not an artist, exactly."

"No big deal," Caitlin speaks up. "You'll figure it out."

"Fantastic!" Trevor is pleased. "This is going to be a *sick* May Day. Even better than when Dispatch played my freshman year."

"Whoa, Trev, that's kind of pushing it, man." Jimmy Reagan, an old tennis camp friend of Trevor's, joins the conversation. "I mean, who are we getting?"

"It will be sick, dude. Trust me," Trevor says.

As they finish up their apples and coffee, Laine has a premonition. *This is the beginning, isn't it?* Like her parents and their friends, she'll sit on this board and that, for ballet and hospitals, arranging balls at the Ritz or auctions at Sotheby's. One good cause after the next. Laine meets Noah's glance, and she smiles warmly. It feels good to be seated in the right chair.

The filmmaker panel at Yale's Independent Film Festival in New Haven is boring the piss out of Chase. He's in an ADD tailspin, which is unfortunate because Chase wanted to enjoy it. This Buddy-Holly-looking hipster cinematographer has been jabbering on for what seems like hours. *Wasn't Matt Damon supposed to be on this panel? Claire Danes? Isn't this her alma mater?* Chase can't keep still, but he's sitting next to Parker, and lately, that's all that matters.

"All right, kids," Nikki says, and interlocks her arms in theirs when the panel ends. "Mr. P is giving us an hour before we get back on that bus. Let's grab some pizza."

At Denardo's, an old Italian joint with a checkered floor and framed shots of dark-suited men on the walls, Nikki orders for the group. The pies arrive and Nikki holds up her thin-crust pancetta slice as if offering communion to Parker and Chase.

"Neither of you appreciates pizza. I mean, Chase wouldn't know the difference between a New York or a Chicago pie, and Parker, do they *have* pizza in Canada?" Nikki bites into her slice and waves a hand at her mouth. "Damn, that's hot! I just burned myself."

"Actually, yes, for your information, we have pizza, hamburgers, *and* hot dogs, all kinds of stuff." Parker blows on hers.

"So, are you guys, like, going out now?" Nikki asks in her sudden and ruthless way.

Parker and Chase grin at each other, mortified.

"You wanna field this one, kid?" Parker asks him.

"We're all really good friends, Nikki," he says, with a politician's slyness and smile. "Aren't we?"

Nikki licks her finger, thinking, her skateboarder's baseball cap to the side, brown eyes dewy in the light of the mirrored restaurant. "We *are* all good friends, but I don't want to get naked with either of you. Care to rephrase, Senator?"

Parker laughs at her roommate. "Gross. But honestly, we are good friends. I've been thinking a lot about it lately. Man, it's crazy; you should see these kids hanging out with that guy Jamie. These girls—parasites, kind of. Most people don't have friends they can really, really trust."

"You still hanging out with that Glendon kid?" Nikki asks.

Parker has told Nikki the basics: that Jamie's alone in a pool house, his parents are abroad, his friends are eccentric, he seems wealthy, he's sweet and crazy. But Chase knows Nikki asked Parker what happened Valentine's Day night, and Parker blamed it on bourbon and an empty stomach.

"What, her other boyfriend?" Chase asks, slurping root beer from a frosted mug. It's meant as a joke, but Chase can't hide his distaste for Jamie.

Parker shoots him a look. "Jamie's a good kid. He's just lost, I think."

"Well," Chase says, "in my humble opinion, the kid loses himself. He could do anything. And he holes up there like a rat and tells you sob stories. Poor little rich dude."

"That was a mouthful, Mr. Character Judge," Parker says snidely.

"Okay, be nice to each other," Nikki says.

On their way to the bus, they pass a lady lounging on the stoop of a closed-down florist. Her Philadelphia Eagles windbreaker and sweatpants are insufficient for March, and soiled. Chase tosses a dollar bill in the cardboard box but the lady doesn't thank him. Suddenly, her head nods up dramatically.

"Yeah," she groans, and the three of them balk at her voice.

She's probably forty, but seems a hundred. The corners

of her mouth are crusty with spit, and her glazed eyes are half closed.

"Shit, that lady is *fucked* up," Nikki says. "What do you think she's on?"

"I don't know. But let's get out of here." Parker picks up the pace.

And as they walk in silence, she thinks back five or six years. To a windstorm that woke her one night, and her father slack-jawed on the downstairs couch. An infomercial for polarized sunglasses. She asks her father if he's awake. He doesn't answer, but his eyes aren't shut, either. He groans and stares at the TV. A pint of ice cream is fully melted on the coffee table. She waits for him to snap out of it but he just nods. She isn't old enough to know what's going on, but she's old enough to know that she doesn't want to know.

Boys Varsity Hockey has reached the finals of the New England Hockey Tournament. Wellington faces Avon Old Farms, an all-guy school known more for athletics than academics.

Nikki, Delia, Greg, and a few other students have made the trip to support the team. The rink is packed with fans. Laine points out the Boston College coach next to the Harvard coach. A few rows closer, pro scouts take notes. Greg shakes his head, saying he should have played hockey. The crowd erupts as Wellington takes the lead 2–1 in the first period. The flock of painted faces, including Laine's, cheers as the Wellington team skates off the ice toward the locker room. Caitlin painted a green "#7," Noah's number, on Laine's cheekbone.

"What are the blue lines?" Delia asks. She's never seen a hockey game and she's peppering Laine with questions.

"It's for offsides," Laine shouts over the crowd. "The offensive team can't be in front of those lines without the puck."

"Like soccer, I get it." Delia is a quick learner.

Caitlin leans into Laine. "I heard you're going to Thailand with Noah for break."

Delia and Nikki are shocked; their mouths drop. "Get out!" says Nikki.

Laine is speechless with embarrassment. She shrugs.

Delia pinches Laine with affection. "That is so cool. You're going to have the greatest time, my God. Where are you going?"

"To Hua Hin?" Laine says as if asking a question.

"Beautiful," Caitlin says, endorsing the venture in her senior-girl way.

Noah doesn't see action until the last horn sounds and he's celebrating with the team on center ice. Wellington wins, and Brian Leetch Jr. wins the tournament MVP award. Like his father, he's headed to the New York Rangers.

Wellington fans jump over the boards onto the ice. Laine waves at Noah from the bleachers. The other girls pounce on her.

"You go out there, girl!" Delia says.

"Get down on that ice and congratulate him," Nikki says sternly.

So Laine makes her way down and hops over the boards, looking back every few minutes. She skates to center ice in blue Pumas.

"Congrats!" Laine yells to him. "You did it!"

Noah, who's been screaming with his teammates, catches his breath, amazed she came down here. "Well, I didn't actually do much, but what the hell." Noah notices the seven on Laine's cheek. "I love the war paint! Thank you."

Laine glides awkwardly into Noah's chest. She puts her arms around his waist and squeezes him.

"You're welcome," she says, and buries her head in his chest pads.

The vapor of ice gets into the lungs. Hidden away in the wings of the rink, an old guy waits with working-class patience on top of a chugging Zamboni. He'll ride the machine in circles and melt the scars of the game away once the kids clear out. His mustache is mustard-yellow with nicotine. His Shetland sweater was hand-knit by his wife. He rubs gnarled hands together, exhales steam.

He watches a girl in blue shoes hug her guy in his bulky

equipment. The Zamboni driver gets a pang through his torso, a spear of memory from his own adolescence. A redhead named Mary met him at the train station when he came back from Fort Dix, and her breath smelled like strawberries and cream, and her neck smelled like dime-store perfume. Her eyes took him in in the same way this blonde is looking at number 7: hungry, abashed, vulnerable. He married Mary and they got old together, and she died last year. He still talks to her as if she were present, when he makes eggs in his kitchen or draws a bath at night. Or now. He mutters in the icy dark: "Look at those kids, Mary. God, remember that?"

14

After yet another snowstorm, Sunday dawns with warmth. And the world melts. The trees are dark and slick. Parker takes Moses for a long walk, and sets out for Jamie's. Moses loves the woods; he strains at the leash when he catches a squirrel's scent. He's beautiful, muscular, and native.

"Hold *on*." She laughs when he pulls too hard. "You can't go anywhere without me, Mo."

She's walking up the drive to the pool house when the back door of the main house opens. Jamie stands there in black jeans, shirtless, dark circles under his eyes. He looks awful.

"Halt. Who goes there?" he asks dully in his Brit twang.

She can't tell if he's kidding. "It's me."

He smiles like a diamond. "I miss you, baby."

She smiles back, unsure. "I miss you, too."

"I cannot play today, luvvy. Me and the big man are havin' a li'l chitchat. Quality time. Chess."

"You play chess?" she asks conversationally.

"No. I dream of murder." He says this with his eyes wide as quarters, and serious, his pupils flush to the rim of the iris.

Parker stands there, and can hear the branches of trees dripping, and the eaves melting. She has no idea what to say, or where to go from here. She wants to be in her room. She wants to be anywhere else.

And then he starts laughing, clutching his skinny ribs, and giving her a wink-wink. "Oh, luvvy, your face!" he exclaims. "Did I scare you? *Did* I?"

She laughs too, and it feels good to break that tension. "You did scare me, Jamie! You fucker."

"Oh, I love you, Park," he says casually, taking her breath away—again. "Listen," he continues swiftly. "Run up to the pool house, there's a whole bottle of candy, fresh from FedEx. Take what you like. You got your break comin' up, don'tcha, luv? Stock up, then, be a good girl."

"Thanks, Jamie. I mean, I don't need to take any, I just came to say hi," she says disingenuously.

"I bought 'em special for you."

"God, thanks."

"Where's Chase?"

Parker shrugs guiltily. "Don't know."

"You going home to Canada for the duration, then, luv?"

"Yeah," she lies.

Suddenly, George appears behind Jamie. He's bigger, taller, than Parker realized. He's wearing that Japanese robe, and his gray hair is pulled into a ponytail. He disappears without speaking.

"What are you gettin' up to today?" Jamie asks.

But George calls out something unintelligible from another room, and Jamie winces.

"I gotta run. I'll see you soon." He waves like a little kid, crumpling his hand. He closes the door, grinning like a clown.

"Oh my God," Parker actually says out loud, trying to process the strange scene.

Moses looks up, wanting to know what's going on.

"Come with me," she tells her dog.

Parker trudges to the pool house. Moses is digging holes in the snow. He stares at her when she opens the door. His feet are too muddy.

"Stay put," she says, looping the leash around a sapling. "I'll be back in two seconds."

In the dark efficiency, she sifts through manila envelopes, books on voodoo and terrorists and Mayans, empty packs of smokes. She hears pills in a bottle—there, she finds the FedEx packet and doles out some medicine. Puts it in her pocket.

A light clicks on and Parker freezes.

"This help?" George is standing with Moses at the top of the stairs. "Your buddy here was on his way down to the road." George scratches Moses's chin.

Parker can't find words. "Oh God."

"Here," he says, holding out the leash, wet from having been dragged. "So how old are you?" George leans against the threshold.

"I'm, uh, I'm sixteen." Parker kneels down and pets Moses.

"Wild time, isn't it?" George doesn't wait for an answer. "When I was sixteen, I was in Belgium, at the Fissoneaux School for Boys. Dropping acid and getting paddled."

"That sounds . . . interesting," she says.

"Life is interesting, isn't it?" He stares at her. "You must be present, and see what it offers to you. Be alive."

Parker jiggles the pills. "Okay," she says uncertainly.

He smiles brightly then. "You seem like a nice girl. A really nice girl." George salutes Parker and starts to head down the steps. He looks back and nods at Moses. "I heard about your rescue mission from Jamie. Many would have left him for dead. You're a nice girl."

Parker stands there, as Moses whimpers and pulls at her. He wants to go back to school. She waits till George's footfalls are gone. Parker doesn't know what George is to Jamie—a friend, or an enemy. He might be Jamie's faux uncle, or lover, or jailkeeper. His trust fund or his nightmare. He's an archetype, a citizen of human society, that she's meeting for the first time.

Noah and Laine take a cab to New Haven right before spring break. They see Dr. Janner, a tall Scandinavian woman, and Noah goes in first while Laine flips through a *Newsweek* in the pristine waiting room. They each get a Havrix vaccine for hepatitis A, and a prescription for Vivotif Berna, capsules to swallow the first few days they arrive in Thailand to prevent typhoid fever.

"Ow," Noah says as they scuff down the slushy sidewalk.

"Oh, come on." Laine smirks. "You baby. That didn't hurt."

"I'm delicate!" Noah jokes.

"It wasn't more than a mosquito sting," Laine says. But the truth is, she likes the pinprick of anticipation. She touches it covertly.

Noah is tempted to nip into an Irish dive bar or a four-star hotel, just to scratch a notch in the boarding-school getting-over bedpost, but he knows Laine won't. And he's happy just to sit in the backseat of the cab back to school, their thighs touching.

"My mom really likes your mom," Noah says, as the cab enters the decrepit periphery of this New England city.

"Thank God, right?" Laine says, folding up her woolen scarf to make a pillow against the window.

The mothers talked on the phone like two diplomats designing a difficult truce, Mirielle with a Hendricks martini, looking at the lavender horizon of New York City and petting her cat, Guggenheim, and Polly in a chintz robe as dusk fell in snowy clumps on the Greenwich house, scribbling down information—flight numbers and hotel rooms and times and dates. But the trip was ultimately okayed, with separate rooms and sincere chaperoning.

God knows, both families are board certified for social standing. The Michonnes' friends are friends with the Hunts' friends. Once Lucien sat in on a meeting where Philip investigated acquiring a couture house run by a bipolar Japanese designer who will remain nameless. Polly and Mirielle sit on the same board for autistic kids, throwing the New York City Opera bash every April. They go to the same bistro on the Upper East Side, eat the same coq au vin there, and drink the same Bordeaux.

Laine is sleeping. Noah watches. The cab jiggles over ruts and potholes as they ride through the New Haven wasteland. The movement of the vehicle eventually parts Laine's legs a few inches. She's wearing a kilt and wool socks, and Noah can't breathe when he catches sight of the creamy inside of that leg.

You're killing me, girl.

After that day, the trip becomes real. They both have a scar as proof. They count the days till they leave Wellington for their homes, and then they have to wait some more for the departure date.

Polly sits Laine down one night in the parlor. She hands her a Bergdorf bag sprouting tissue paper. Inside are a red alligator passport folder and a Lily beach cover-up.

"Mom! Thank you," says Laine, and kisses her cheek.

Her mother waves it off. "You'll be good, Laine," Polly says with worried eyes.

Laine *will* be good. The last thing she wants to do is add to her mother's fatigue and worry. Laine's sister Christine, in ninth grade at Greenwich Academy, has taken up cutting herself with glass or safety pins. Polly's hands and heart are full with that emergency. In fact, Polly thinks Christine has been safe this week, but Laine found a balled-up tennis sock in a drawer with fresh stripes of blood.

"I will be good, Mother."

"Oh, you're going to have a lovely time, sweetheart. I bet you're so excited."

"I am," Laine lies. Because she dreads the trip as much as she looks forward to it. All she and Noah have done is kiss. There's no way he'll leave it at that for the span of Thailand. In Laine's mind, sex is still the price of love, not the essence of it. She isn't ready. The territory of sexuality is as foreign as Asia; she can look at a map and understand where it is, but she can't imagine what it's like to be there.

Back in January, she wished Noah would leave her alone. Now this is exactly what she fears. That he'll meet her brick wall, abandon all hope, and leave her. Alone.

15

Tuesday, dawn. Time to go.

Philip takes her in his chauffeured town car on his way to work. It's dark, silent, and town cars slide like stingrays along plowed Greenwich roads on their way to Wall Street, headlights lit like hungry eyes. At Noah's building, Philip brings her luggage to the sleepy doorman, and kisses Laine on the cheek.

"Bring me a souvenir, my dear," he says.

"You know I will," she answers, and he watches her disappear into the warm mahogany lobby through the revolving door. He stands for another minute, watching the door twirl and then stop.

As she ascends in the elevator, operated by a guy in a maroon suit, her mouth gets dry. The Michonnes know about her screwup at 60 Thompson, although Laine doesn't know how much they heard. They were really nice to her at the wedding, but this is different.

The gold door opens now into the Michonnes' penthouse, and Laine stands there, knees knocking like those of an orphan sent to a new home.

"Well, hello!" Mirielle says, and hugs the child, who she imagines might seem forlorn because of the hour, or who might be intimidated about going to Asia with another family. "Noah!" Mirielle calls out in her chiming voice.

Noah appears, hair sticking up, and he rubs his eyes. "Hey, Laine," he says in a scratchy and tender tone.

His mother likes them as a couple, she has a good feeling about them, and she claps her hands, making her floorlength Etro robe flutter. "Who wants coffee?" she asks.

Parker presses her forehead against the plane's porthole, gazing at the blue yonder.

The plane lands hard. The airfield is fringed with palmettos, the sun sparkling like emeralds in their leaves. Waiting at baggage claim is a boy she loves. As she approaches him, she withholds a smile. His white Havaianas are dirty, his Parliaments jammed into his shirt pocket, a John Deere hat pulled over his eyes. She walks up to his grungy, nervous Southern ass.

"Take this stupid hat off," she says, pulling it off and kissing him.

They race and then slow down and race and slow down, trying to trip each other, crossing the parking lot. Outside, her hair burns red, and Chase is bewildered. *She's here. She's here, across the state line, in my town.* He throws her bag into the bed of the pickup and opens her door, bows. On her side of the dash is a magnolia blossom he picked before he left his house.

Parker already loves it here. They drive through lush country. They pass through an all-black neighborhood on the periphery of Charleston, where an old man shaves in a rusty basin on his porch, a shard of mirror attached to the post. They drive through the city, and Chase points out where his dad works, where his nursery school was, where a kid he knew got murdered, where he played Little League. The buildings are pastel, loaded with hurricane shutters. Tropical vines twirl around iron stoop railings.

A church has a bloodred steeple. A white-haired African-American woman rakes its yard.

"That's where my parents got married."

"For real?" Parker says as it slides by; for one moment she sees into the mouth of the building, and it's dark.

"Yeah, my mom was nineteen. But that was, like, normal."

"Did she go to college?"

"Hell, no." Chase laughs. "She's a wife."

"He wouldn't let her?"

"She never considered it. She was raised to be beautiful and charming and to take care of people."

Parker, whose mom has a PhD, imagines a different life. "Got it."

"Not like he would have encouraged her, though, if she *had* wanted to. He's a bully, dude. He gets to hit the law office, charm the dollars off every sucker who walks into the room, drink bourbon down at Ganson Mill with his cronies after work, and come home to baked catfish and red beans, steaming hot. He's got it made, but I bet my mom wouldn't mind one less remark a week about how she overcooks the lamb."

Chase's voice sours when talking about his dad. It's a battle, one that can't have a winner. A Dobbs man is always right.

"Um, my brother's home too," he adds without pleasure. "Just for tonight, he and his girlfriend are heading to Negril tomorrow."

Parker grins. "You think I can't handle it?"

Chase makes a funny face and shrugs, but says nothing.

She rubs his thigh. She's terrified. She's the lanky half Lithuanian, part Greek, and part Irish Canadian brunette whose family took out loans for school and who probably votes against every single value and desire the Dobbs have, and whose face is all angles and whose dowry is one vintage motorcycle and some turquoise bracelets. She's the polar opposite of the aristocratic and submissive and classically beautiful teenage bride.

The house is butter yellow with white pillars, and nubs are bursting on the azalea shrubs flanking it. A Boykin Spaniel races down the stoop stairs. Mr. Dobbs stands at the door, hands on hips, a smile on his age-freckled face.

"Hey, Dad, this is Parker."

"Well, well, well," Randall murmurs. "We are *so* happy to have you here, Miss Parker."

"So happy to be here, Mr. Dobbs," she says, and steps up to shake his hand.

It's like climbing to heaven and meeting a god.

They proceed into the foyer, where a narrow Oriental rug leads them to the kitchen. Mrs. Dobbs faces the counter, sticking mint sprigs into glasses. Her black hair is pulled into a bun, her belted dress a relic of the forties. Parker's heart sinks through the floor. Then Mrs. Dobbs turns around.

"You must be Parker!" she drawls.

"Nice to meet you, Mrs. Dobbs."

"Why don't we head out onto the porch and you can tell me all about your trip, sweetheart," she says, carrying a tray decoupaged with butterflies. The glasses of sweet tea shiver. Her hands tremble. Her face, in its wide-eyed deer-like beauty, is fearful.

Mrs. Dobbs is shy.

They sip and small-talk while March sun comes through the screen, crosshatching their faces and arms. Where the floor meets the wall is the skeleton of a gecko, and Parker can't help staring. Chase smiles; she located the shred of mortality in the room. Things are going decently, when Reed and Courtney walk in, hand in hand.

Introductions. Everyone is polite, smiling and smiling. Reed eventually steers Courtney out of the room, his hands gripping the tops of her shoulders. Parker looks worried; Courtney is every single thing that Parker cannot become. Blond, with a cheerleader's disposition, tanned curvy legs like basted chicken, a drawl thick as crude oil, and no ambition but to love Reed and make him happy.

"Why don't I show you your room, Park, and you can unpack and stuff," Chase says.

The hardwood floor is scratched by the dog, and the dog before this dog, and the dog before that one. The shelves are crammed with books on the Civil War—or rather, the War of Northern Aggression, as it's known down here—and Rosamunde Pilcher novels and seashell guides. Parker sits on the bed and sighs. Chase sits next to her, and with nicotine-stained fingers, he gathers up her lustrous hair and holds it like auburn silk.

The Michonnes and Laine take a train from Bangkok to Hua Hin, a three-hour ride in modern cars that have blue stripes painted on their metallic exteriors. The wooden seats have red cushions, and the locomotive clacks past coconut farms and wet jungle, the gold ears of Buddhist temples poking out of the landscape.

Laine feels like a child, nose pressed to the glass. She's never been anywhere that looks like this or smells like this or steams like this. The outside air is dense with heat, and the cars are air-conditioned.

"What do you think?" Noah asks her.

She smiles back. "It's *amazing*."

They're both stale, aching from the journey. But this is worth it. Laine looks at Noah, his worldly eyes, his linen shirt, and she tries it out in her head: *Noah, my boyfriend. My boyfriend, Noah. Let me introduce you to Noah; he's my boyfriend.*

The train takes a pit stop in a village where Thai kids play tag with a red ribbon. Noah and his dad get out, come back with plastic bowls of cold mango slices covered with coconut custard for everyone. Laine tries a bite, and Noah has to look away. *Her little mouth, the orange-magenta fruit.*

When they get to the Alteena, their avant-garde hotel, Thai porters take their luggage. The Michonnes have rented the villa, a building separate from the hotel, for the week. The parents have the suite upstairs, and Noah and Laine have separate rooms downstairs. On the roof is a white-washed patio with a thatched awning. And the building is punctuated at its base by coconut trees and orchids.

"We're home!" Mirielle calls out, joking, and lays down her vintage Gucci duffel. Somehow the bags under her eyes don't prevent her from remaining her glamorous self. When the Thai proprietor emerges from the beachside to welcome them, Mirielle answers him in French and they talk like old friends.

Laine lies on her bed, feeling deeply, deeply weary. The rafters are teak, and the walls are white. On the dresser is a lotus, its white petals curving over the yellow center. It's closed. Her eyes close. Noah knocks and whispers. It makes her nervous and she pretends to be asleep until he goes away.

She slops about in her dream. She's on a train, and she keeps trying to turn on the light but can't find the chain. She hears it; it jangles in the dark. Suddenly she realizes the floor is slippery, or moving. Although she doesn't want to touch whatever is down there, she has to know. So she reaches to her ankles and almost gags; snakes writhe around her feet, climb her calves by twisting around them.

She sits up, and it takes a second to clear her vision. She's in a room. It's her room. The floor is wood, and the lotus flower is open.

She walks outside, where dark clouds let sabers of light fall onto the sand. The water sparkles like diamonds. There he is, Noah, dragging his thighs through the surf to come to her, his hair slicked, skin shining. She meets him before he clears the waterline, and suds clean their feet. She puts her arms around him, her clothes instantly damp, her face warm against his cool, goose-bumped neck.

The first night is easygoing. Betsy makes shrimp and grits with bacon gravy, the way her grandmother made it. Randall asks Parker about her parents, where she grew up, what she's studying, and what she wants to do after college. His voice booms, and Parker stays composed and answers his questions. He makes outlandish jokes that lighten the mood, but that manage to confuse Parker. *They seem happy as a family.*

On the wall, an oil portrait of a man in the ruffles of a nineteenth-century overcoat bears a resemblance to Randall, and is, in fact, a British ancestor.

"I think that's enough interrogation, darling," Betsy says quietly and with charm. She takes a silver serving spoon—initials etched into the handle's thumb—to the dessert. "Let the poor dear eat her rhubarb crumble."

"I've been monopolizing you," Randall drawls in his massive voice. "I'm a curious man, that's all. And you are far too attractive to be dating this scoundrel."

Chase laughs as if he's heard the jokes a thousand times before. "Yeah, you're a real prize, Pop," he says sarcastically.

Reed and Courtney watch *American Pie* for the hundredth time after dinner, lounging on the couch, Reed's UVA hat turned backward, his jaw blond with fuzz. As always, his hand rests on Courtney's leg. Everyone got along at dinner, and Chase asks Reed to shove over so he and Parker can watch.

Reed kicks Chase in the knee, joking but not really. "Go find your own fucking movie." He grins.

Chase takes this kick. "Come on. Just move."

"You weren't listening."

"It's actually my DVD," Chase says.

"You're not going to be that much of a baby," Reed says. "Take Parker Posey and find your own spot."

Parker looks down, but not fast enough to avoid seeing Chase's red cheeks.

Chase picks up a magazine and clumsily throws it at his brother. Reed gets up, has Chase hard against the wall so fast that no one knows what's happening. Reed holds Chase's head by his hair and bangs it once—with some restraint—and hisses at him to get out of the room. Courtney and Parker are, for a moment, equalized, as they look at each other in alarm and apology, a millisecond that communicates a timeless message between women.

"Cannot *wait* for you to leave this house," Chase says under his breath as he straightens his shirt and leaves, Parker trailing him.

They lie on Chase's bed, whose mahogany bedposts cast shadows on the duvet.

"He's just always been like that," Chase says in a small voice.

"I know, I know he has," Parker says, soothing him, rubbing his chest. "I know."

They spend a couple hours like that, suspended in affection.

The light is low; a palmetto leaf touches the window screen. A ceiling fan turns. Outside it's cooled, and crickets and frogs make ragged noises. When Betsy's footsteps approach, Parker jumps into the wicker chair, and Chase sits up, rakes his hair.

"Just want to say good night, my dears," she purrs. Which means: *You two must separate.*

Parker stands. "I do have to get to sleep. I'm exhausted from flying and everything."

"Well, sweet dreams, Parker. We're thrilled you're with us."

She's lying in the dark in leggings and a Joan Jett tank top, a shaft of light coming under the door. She's dozing off when Chase slips into the room without knocking. He's got a plastic cup of sherry.

"It's the only thing I haven't tapped in their liquor cabinet," he whispers.

She giggles, and they lie in bed, in the dark, slumped against the headboard, sharing the cup.

At one point, Parker rubs his head: "Your brother is a sadist, Chase."

"Tell me what that is again?"

"It's a fancy word for asshole."

He stifles laughter, then kisses her sherry-sweet mouth. He takes the cup out of her hand.

"What are you doing?" she singsongs quietly, knowing what he's doing.

They both feel loose, and hold each other tight. They take a long time to kiss. They draw it out. There's no hurry. Their bodies are hard against each other, but the bed is soft. They fall into a slow ecstasy, a place neither has ever visited. This is better than what they've had before. Rubbing her palms on his chest, Parker feels that she knows him finally.

She wakes up to morning light coming through drapes. She's wearing underwear and that's it. Her hair is tangled, the red cup gone, and she loves Chase so much it hurts.

She puts on her jean skirt and T-shirt, walks barefoot to the kitchen to see if he's up and making breakfast. She's starving. But it's only Randall, sitting at the table, turned away from his newspaper and staring at the floor. He looks at Parker and doesn't seem surprised, even though he looks at the old Rolex on his thick arm.

"Aren't you a little early?" he drawls in a flat voice. "It's only quarter after six."

Parker is surprised. "Oh, gosh," she says. "I had no idea. I'm usually a late sleeper." Now she doesn't know what to do, her shirt slipped off one shoulder, her plastic bangles mutely clacking as she pushes hair behind her ear.

Randall looks out the window as if a headless horseman might arrive. He seems much older in the blue morning.

"Chase must know that I think well of him," he says. Then he looks to Parker like a boy looks to his mother for answers.

"Oh," Parker stammers. "He does," she lies.

"I love that boy. He just gets under my skin. He's stubborn."

"Of course," Parker says now, and gets a glass for water.

"I hope he doesn't hold it all against me. You can tell him that."

"I will."

But that's all he says, and he stares at the floor. Parker slips back to her room. At ten, she smells sausage and coffee. She nervously tries the kitchen again, and this time Betsy is clipping roses to put in a vase, and Randall is heartily stirring links in a skillet and telling jokes in his immortal voice.

Thailand is amazing. The people at the hotel are brilliant and sweet, and the sea stretches from their rooms' windows like rippled crystal. Noah and Laine eat tiger prawns with plum sauce, tuna with ginger and Thai lime, and pumpkin warmed in coconut milk. Noah meets the chef's son, Badinton, who shows Noah the underbelly of the place, the kitchen and the staff's housing. Noah sees a dirty magazine, with Thai lettering and naked Asian women on the cover, on someone's bamboo dresser. As if he needed any more provocation.

He points to the porn rag and says to Badinton, who has an almost working knowledge of English: "Nice literature."

Badinton makes a confused face.

Noah gives a thumbs-up. "Good book," he says clearly.

This time Badinton grins, nodding—one seventeen-year-old to another. "Good book," he manages.

The place is sultry, decadent. One night they watch a Dance of Welcome, where women in red gowns and bare feet move on a wood stage. Their golden fingernails curve out, like claws. The women smile in an innocent and almost maternal way, but those talons inspire in Noah a kaleidoscope of yearnings.

"What did you think?" he asks Laine as they walk the path to the house that night.

"Oh my God," she says, holding his hand and swinging it. "Totally amazing."

But then he gets a kiss and a closed door.

Today his mom meets with the painter Ismet Thammasat.

That's one of the reasons the family is making the trip. Laine and Noah sit in the breakfast room, sipping iced tea with condensed milk, and watch Mirielle talk with Ismet. They speak French, and consonants flutter like moths. Ismet wears paint-smudged pants, and his braid dangles down his back. Noah's mother says something and Ismet laughs, slender hands clasped together. Everyone loves Noah's mother.

"Ismet's going to take us through the Floating Market," Mirielle says when she walks over to their table, her kaftan swaying. "Shall we?"

They drive in Ismet's Toyota Tiger, a truck with four-wheel drive for muddy roads. Thai pop music plays from his radio, and wet leaves drag against the vehicle's sides. The sun is high when they reach the market, and they all wear sunglasses and wander the docks, gazing at this clustering of long-tail boats. The hulls bloom with lettuce heads, coconuts, lemongrass bunches, strawberries, mangos, pine-apples, cords of asparagus, and rose apples.

Noah watched a monkey family yesterday, and now he feels like a primate himself. He's never been this out of control, and he blames the perfume and motion and silk here. The smoke and the fruit. He wants to lose his mind. When he can, he herds Laine into the shade of a shed. He kisses her lips. She seems nervous and aloof, as always, but he presses on. Right there, tucked in shadow, out of sight of his mother and Ismet, Noah presses his leg between her thighs, and his chest to hers. The last straw is a grasp of the ass. She pulls away, condemns him with a look, and starts running down the boardwalk.

When he catches up, she plays it off.

"Ha-ha, you can't catch me," she says, keeping her hand away from his as he tries to hold it.

"Did I scare you?" he asks as they walk through beautiful chaos.

"What are you talking about?" She smiles, as if nothing happened.

16

Parker and Chase have poked around town, run errands for his mother, watched movies, and bidden Reed good-bye. It's raining in Charleston. They rock on porch chairs, sip sweet tea. Drops fall on the road and on the azalea leaves and on the umbrellas of people walking by.

Parker is feeling pleasantly woozy but in control. Since she's been here, she's meted out to herself with restraint the pills she brought. When she was little, she stole sugar cubes from a jar on the kitchen table, sucked them until every grain dissolved, her spit thickening in her throat. Even then she knew to hold back, to enjoy the melting sweetness in her mouth, the secret, and the moments after.

"I don't know," Parker muses now, as they discuss Wellington. "I maybe made a mistake. I shouldn't be there; it's not the right place."

Chase can't help but be offended. If she hadn't gone to Wellington, they wouldn't be sitting here, watching a dog shake water from his coat. They wouldn't have spent secret hours in the past few days in dark rooms, figuring things out.

Parker senses this. "But I'm glad I made that mistake or else I wouldn't be here."

"You're just saying that," he drawls, tipping back his glass, bare feet on a wicker stool. "Anyway. I hear you. The place blows. It's just a cold, snobby, capitalist factory. But we're not there right now."

"We're not there," Parker agrees, smiling wistfully. "I like where we are."

If only they both could have left it at that.

The rain clears, leaving the world sweet. And they suddenly feel restless. When Cobb calls that afternoon, tells them to get down to Sandy's river house for beers and bonfires, they perk up. Jeremiah picks them up in an ancient Volvo, which they park by the loading dock. Sandy's family is big and boisterous, and they live in the center of Charleston, spending little time at the river house. His dad doesn't mind if the kids hang out there. Already a good blaze is on.

"Chaser-oo!"

Sandy's sitting by the fire, his thunder thighs in damp bathing shorts, grease stains on his Johnny's Bait Shop shirt, his hat turned back. With the red of the fire on his cherubic cheeks, he looks like a mischievous angel. This is one of Chase's favorite friends, and they high-five.

Chase introduces Parker around, and they get handed Natural Lights in koozies. Cold beer, twilight, good friends.

"How you likin' our town? Chase showing you around?" asks Sandy with politeness, even as his friends shoot beer bottles that they fling into the sky, the shards raining over the river, scaring an egret from the reeds. Chase's crew has always been a mixed bag of stoner surfers and renegade rednecks. Just like at Wellington, Chase navigates both worlds without blinking.

"I love it here," Parker answers. "Never really been south before this."

"Ever had an oyster roast?" Sandy asks.

"Definitely not."

"Oh, you're in for a treat," he assures her, his Santa Claus belly serving as confirmation of his status as connoisseur. "Glad you guys are here. We barely ever get to see Chase during the summer when he goes Kelly Slater on us."

Parker laughs. "He's hardly Kelly Slater," she says, wincing as the twenty-gauge shotgun is fired.

"No shit, darling." Sandy turns to Chase. "Girl tells it like it is, son. 'Bout time somebody smacked you around a bit."

Parker Cole is winning over the South.

181

Night falls, and oysters are loaded on iron racks over the fire. They're covered with wet burlap and left to cook. The keg gets abused, until finally the crew embarks on stands and funnels. Parker and Chase spend time on the beach chairs on the lawn, joking with everyone. Parker mainly watches, ducking as childhood references and stories zing past. It's okay. She sucks down frothy beer. She feels blessed, melting like butter in the alcoholic heat—even as the night blackens and the bats become indecipherable from the sky.

It's when she goes into the house to pee that she sees the Other Crew. They're holding derelict court on the screened porch. The energy is different from the laziness outside. One guy, in a button-down shirt and khaki shorts, hair parted and glossy like a talk-show host's, stands with arms crossed and talks over the conversation. He reminds everyone that his dad owns two yachts, both headed for Race Week in Newport this summer.

"Zip it, Thomas," says a mean-eyed girl sitting on the flagstone floor. "Your dad won't even let you on the boat."

"What are you talking about?" Thomas asks. "I sailed that thing to Block Island and back." He's terribly offended by her disbelief.

That's all Parker hears before closing the door to the loo. But she knew what was going on, due to the stridency of voices and nail-biting and bragging. She opens the medicine cabinet. It's not there. She checks the tub. Then she finds it in the cobalt glass jar of Q-tips: a bag of coke with a dusty pen cap. Like a bloodhound, she smelled it. She's only done it a few times with Jamie, but from the first second of getting high, she'd known she loved it. She runs water and takes stolen bumps, then washes her nostrils for fear of being caught.

Outside, she luxuriates in manic heart thumping. In the dark, she smiles.

"You okay?" Chase says without suspicion, placing his hand on her knee.

"I'm great," she says.

Over the next hours, cars eventually back down the drive, headlights cutting the cedar-shingled house. Gravel crunches as teens carefully steer away. Parker and Chase end up inside. Parker's been *dying* for more. It was almost even: her desire to revive the high and her fear of being suspected for dipping into someone else's treasure. So she had been sitting on her hands around the bonfire, feeling the rush fall away.

As she and Chase make drinks in the kitchen and have a moment alone, she looks slyly at him.

"Guess what the kids out there are doing?"

Chase had sniffed the scent, too, finally. He knows they shouldn't engage, but he wants to do it. "Not so hard to imagine," he says.

She tries not to seem imploring, and shrugs. "Should you ask?"

He smiles back. They're comrades in acquisition. "Yeah."

The anticipation on her face makes him uneasy, but he buries his instincts.

They sit around the glass porch table with four others, doing rails, jabbering about glacier meltdown and Angelina Jolie and crawfish. Around eleven, Chase calls home to say he'll get a ride later from Jeremiah's dad. And if he doesn't come back, that means he and Parker stayed at Sandy's. His mother says she doesn't like the sound of that, and Chase says they'll almost definitely be home, and not to worry.

"What are you doing out there anyway?" Betsy asks suspiciously.

"Watching movies, Mom," Chase answers without hesitation.

He gets off the phone quickly, guiltily.

"How'd that go?" Parker asks apologetically.

"It went," Chase replies.

That's the bottom line of doing late-night business.

Thomas is now in a superhigh funk, glaring at everyone, his neck veins pumping. The mean-eyed girl, Bess, is the line cutter. Sandy asks Parker every little thing about her life and she is more than happy to tell him. And Cobb, Jeremiah, and Chase look frantically and blissfully through a tackle box they found, evaluating each lure and fly.

Jeremiah's brother picks him up around three A.M. Parker and Chase stare at each other, wondering what to do. Chase knows he's already dead, but if they make it home now, there's a chance for redemption.

"We should catch this ride," he says in defeat.

Parker hides her anger and disappointment. There's a mound of powder on the scratched-up glass. But she knows what she'd be called if she insists on staying. She'll be a Fiend. She'll officially have a Problem.

"Okay, cool," she forces out of her mouth, and it sounds fake.

They say good night, and walk to the spears of light coming through the hedge. Jeremiah bumbles ahead, smoking a last cigarette, stomping through weeds. Parker gets claustrophobic as they near the Suburban. She's so high.

"Is there a chance your parents are going to be waiting up for us?" she asks.

Chase stops. He can't lie. "They might. One of them might."

She fidgets with her hair, pulling sections of it. "Shit, babe."

"Are you scared?" he asks.

She nods, her heart hammering, her mouth dry, and her mind scrambled.

"You want to wait it out here?"

"Maybe. It's just that I've never even tried to slip by my parents, and yours are more, well, you know—"

Chase interrupts her. "It's okay."

The silhouettes in the truck are invisible witnesses to this anxiety. Smoke rolls out of the left window. Chase approaches and tells Jeremiah they're going to hold tight.

"No worries, brother," he says, and the vehicle rolls out, its tires heavy on the earth, spewing an occasional rock.

Parker is ashamed for balking, and she takes Chase's hand as they turn toward the house. Chase feels her emotion. He stops.

"I have an idea," he says softly.

Noah wakes up this morning, his hotel sheets tangled and wet.

"Oh, Christ," he mutters, and balls them up for the maid. He wishes he could take them somewhere, but where? The sea? Wash his pornographic dream from his bedding at the beach? That would be normal.

He gets in the shower to scald off the fantasy that woke him. He orients himself to reality: *She didn't lie next to me like that, she didn't touch me like that, she didn't kiss me there, she didn't say what I wanted to hear, we weren't together.* When he turns the faucet handle, he feels better aligned with the truth.

But when he and Laine are in town, watching an elephant

ritual where the animals spin and stop, spin and stop, trunks gesturing to the crowd and the papaya trees and the sun, he fills up again with desire. He can barely concentrate on the animals. Laine is wearing a white dress, and the frill trembles in the breeze as if someone is blowing on it.

He's so distracted that any little question, like *Are you hot? Want to go swimming? Are you thirsty? Want some of these bracelets to bring back?* he has to ask her to repeat.

"You're in space, mister," she says, swinging his hand.

She wonders, meanwhile, if he knows she's sorry. She knows what he wants, and that it hurts not to get it. Sometimes, in bed, she gives herself a redressing. As if she were a child to be scolded, who should repent. *Try,* she says. *Just try.*

But when she sees him, she freezes. She's not ready.

Back at the villa, Noah's changing into Vilebrequin swim trunks. The bed is made, a lotus blossom curled on the pillow. He almost had sex once, and it was horrific. It was last Christmas break in the city, and he tries not to remember it, but he can't suppress the vision right now. It was at his friend Alexander's apartment on Spring Street, and Alex's parents were on a trip. No one went very far, but it was far enough.

Alex, Noah, and Francis used Alex's sister's room, and the girl—a Puerto Rican classmate of Alex's who was drunk and stoned, as they all were, and at the beginning seemed to be having more fun than anyone—cried after they had all done what they had done. Alex and Francis took her downstairs to put her in a cab and to talk her down from her hysteria (as well as get her by the doorman) while Noah painstakingly made the bed, and suddenly threw up, barely reaching the bathroom in time.

Now, here in Thailand, he looks in the mirror, at his chest and freckled cheekbones, his hands—and wonders why we're made the way we're made. It's rather painful. We're just built to want so much.

He meets Laine by the waterline. Herons leave their shadow on the sands. The day is glittering and hot.

"What took you so long?" Laine kids, splashing water at him.

"Whatever, you're the one who's always late," he says, almost unable to look at her in that tobacco-brown bikini. It's tiny, and her torso shines with salt water.

He splashes her back, and they engage in full-on warfare. At a certain point, he grabs her and swings her around, and then she struggles out of his grasp and splashes him again.

"You're asking for it," he says menacingly.

She squeals and tries to move away in the hip-deep water. He lunges for her, wraps his strong arms around her bare waist. "Gotcha!" he says.

He turns her around and kisses her, under the blue sky. She lets his body press against hers, and kisses him back.

When he groans, though, she shrugs out of his embrace.

"God!" she says, crossing her arms, and she looks ashamed and furious.

Noah stands there, hands on hips, embarrassed, too. "You know, Laine, it's not like we're doing anything crazy here. This is kind of par for the course for couples, you know what I mean?" He sounds much more bitter and ugly than he wants to sound, but he can't help it.

She stares. Those deep-set eyes, the dimples, the wet hair, his jaw. She's been waiting for this handsome face to look at her the way it's looking now, with disappointment, and then to look away, like he's doing now, with resignation. It's crazy that it should happen here, in the ocean, in Southeast Asia. She's getting read her rights. It's over.

She always listened to girls talk about guys—*you gotta give up something, you gotta satisfy him enough so that blah blah blah, you have to do this and you have to do that.* It terrified her. She'd nod dumbly at the conversation, and dread her future. For some reason she's a freak, she's "frigid," she's abnormal, and now she's been found out.

"I'm *sorry*," she says.

But then she breaks into snotty-nosed bawling, the most violent crying Noah's seen since his little sister broke her arm on a trampoline. He looks at Laine with alarm as she hiccups and wails.

"Babe, it's okay," he tries eventually, but she stands

there, arms crossed and chest heaving. He puts a wet arm around her shoulders, hugs her sideways like a skittish friend. "Really."

This makes her cry harder, and he pats her back, totally lost.

She straightens up. Looks at him with bloodshot eyes. "But I love you," she says.

She might as well have just said that she was president of the United States, or something equally insane. It takes Noah a few stunned moments to process. Is this happening? Is this girl, sleek and trembling in this Asian sea, opening her hands to him, and giving him everything?

"Laine, we'll go as slow as you want. I will never ask you to do something you don't want to do."

"I don't know what's wrong with me," she says in a voice scratchy from crying.

"Oh my God, nothing's wrong with you," Noah says, and means it.

Nothing at all. Even if he has to pack his lust into his suitcase and secure it with a gold padlock, she's worth it. He kisses her wet head, and holds her until she slowly and finally stops trembling.

Under a moon haloed by the rumor of rain, Chase and Parker are coming down from their high in Sandy's family's boat, docked in reeds far from the house. Sandy thinks they've left with Jeremiah. It's five in the morning, and their nerves are shot. Parker's lying on the floor with Chase and she's twirling her hair and looking around as if demons might emerge from the cattails.

"What have we done?" she laments.

Chase's arms are crossed behind his head. The milkiest of light is leaking into the night sky from its edges. A bird chirps here and there in the stillness. "Man, we're screwed."

The boat is varnished teak, and they lie in the hull, like fish caught and dragged on board. She rolls into him and huddles there, as if she can find sleep in his body. He rubs her back, still staring at the sky.

"Oh, Park," he says softly, not meaning anything.

They kiss, and it feels good, balm on rough nerves. The pleasure of fooling around is like medicine. They take each other's clothes off slowly. Then he rips her T-shirt by accident, and she takes off one of his socks but forgets the other. She's on top, and they're doing what they haven't done yet. Parker's hurt and disoriented at first, and then nothing hurts either of them. They would look strange to anyone looking down from on high—two naked bodies on a boat docked in the dawn over a river in South Carolina. It's in both of their minds that they shouldn't be doing this without protection, or that he should at the very least pull out at the end, but the end nears, and neither moves, and then the end is here, and he's still inside her.

Later, Jeremiah will know enough to lie when he's called by Mr. Dobbs in the morning, and he'll know enough to jump in the truck and go back down to Sandy's, where he'll find the two lovers glistening with dew, fierce with halitosis, poisoned and too embarrassed to even feel embarrassed. Jeremiah will turn away while they stumble about the hot, sunny boat and get their clothes on, and then Jeremiah will take them home. In a few hours, Chase and Parker will regret so many things, but at the moment they're in a bizarre and dangerous heaven.

Now they fall asleep in the wild.

17

Parker can't stop crying. She's in her room, back at school. Nikki left already for film class, and Parker's missing it—because she can't stop sobbing, and even if she could, her eyes are *scarlet*. She's thinking of Chase's dad screaming in the kitchen, and Parker having to hear it from her guest room. She's thinking of pills she took when Chase wasn't looking. She's staring at her unpacked bags of dirty clothes; she couldn't get it together to wash them. She's got zits on her forehead from not washing her face last night. She spent all her allowance for the rest of the year in South Carolina.

And she's not supposed to get her period for three weeks. That's too long not to know. And her body feels different. Something deep inside is screaming: *There is a beginning in here.* Is she imagining it? Or is this intuition?

So what does Parker do? It's simple. She cuts an Oxy in half with a knife, on her desk. She crushes it with her student ID and rolls a dollar bill to snort it.

She puts Visine in her eyes. Brushes her hair. Sniffles. Changes one dirty shirt for another less dirty shirt. Throws on her rabbit-fur jacket. And goes to film class after all. Walks right in there, the period half over, and sits down with a megawatt smile.

Chase walks briskly through the quad to avoid interaction. He has déjà vu. He pauses and scans his surroundings. He's been here before. Last year. Same weather. Same buildings. Same helplessness. He takes comfort in spring being on the horizon, when he can wear his flip-flops and khaki shorts without getting frostbite. There's no snow now. Just acres of mud.

He's got a really bad taste in his mouth. He keeps seeing his dad's big, red fist balled in anger, spittle flying from his mouth as he shouted at Chase. He managed to mess up again. No one to blame this time.

Then he sees Parker do a line of coke, and touch her fragile nostril after, as it stings. He sees those cattails waving, as they lie there in the boat. The Southern sun coming up red and quickly mellowing to pink, and then to white. He feels her body against his. And he decrees, *Sometimes it's just worth it.*

Chase settles at a library computer; he's researching for

a science paper. He sometimes works better when he gets out of the dank privacy of his room, and today, especially, he just didn't want to be there. But instead of focusing on the Bohr model, in all its molecular glory, he finds himself Googling "drug addiction" and "OxyContin" and "rehab." He'd been tempted to bring it up in Charleston. Her twitchy jaw and extra bathroom trips weren't lost on him. And yesterday in the snack bar, she was in the bathroom and he was digging for loose change in her jacket but found a pill case instead. *How clueless does she think I am?*

"Hey, loser," Nikki whispers seductively in Chase's ear.

Chase tries to close the window. He realizes she's been reading over his shoulder. "Jesus Christ. You scared the shit out of me."

"What you doing up here, looking for a career?"

"Yeah, right," he says. "In a meth lab."

"You're worried?"

Chase doesn't look up. "What do you mean?"

Nikki sits down. "I'm not sure what's going on, Chase, you know? Like, what level she's at. But it is *freaky.*"

"How'd you know?" Chase sits back, relieved to talk to someone, even though this feels like a betrayal.

Nikki laughs sarcastically. "Am I retarded? Every time she goes to that kid's house, she comes back like an extra from *Requiem for a Dream.*"

"Nik, I think she's in some serious shit."

They look at each other. She reaches out and takes his hand. "Do we need to figure something out?" she asks.

Chase nods.

They spend the next half hour reading testimonials of teens whose friends or siblings have overdosed, or who succumbed to addiction and then had to use monster strength to get free. The photographs are of kids in suburban homes, on couches upholstered in velour, with a cat sniffing at them. They wear gold chains, or baseball hats and thermal shirts. They look straight at the camera; they look right through Nikki and Chase.

"I'll say something, Chase. I'm with her every night." Nikki smiles. "If I can get a word in. All she ever talks about is you."

Chase grins. "Let's hope it's not the Oxy talking."

"Since when are you short on confidence?" Nikki punches him.

"Since I realized I'm in way over my head." Chase stands and stretches.

She shakes her head. "Chase, I'll say something to her."

Nikki's been a friend even when he didn't deserve it. "Nah. Let me do it first. I don't want her to think we're all freaked out just yet."

Charvet Bistro is in a converted barn, and patrons eat by candlelight under the eaves. Diners take dusk carriage rides around acres of farmland. The kids are told ghost stories, while adults hear the history of Elias Charvet's land. Hokey, but far enough away from Wellington to put Chase at ease.

"What do you think?" he asks Parker as they're escorted to a corner table.

"Perfect," she says sincerely, her flowered dress swaying as her motorcycle boots clomp across the wood floor.

Parker holds Chase's hand as he small-talks with an elderly couple from Boston at the next table. When his grilled quail appetizer and her fennel-and-feta salad are placed in front of them, they hungrily pick up forks.

Chase's heart is racing as Parker rehashes play practice. He laughs convincingly enough when she imitates Jorgen doing Romeo in a Swedish accent, but his mind is elsewhere. Chase lets her speak. He lumps mashed potatoes and pheasant together. He eats, but nervous nausea has crept up.

He imagines saying what he needs to say, and then she dumps her dinner on his head, steals a handle of Jack Daniel's from the bar, hops on a horse outside the restaurant, and rides away while giving him the finger. The other diners will smirk. He'll be alone at midnight, bottles of wine toppled on the table, an ashtray of Marlboro butts. And his old man yanking him by the collar.

"So do you want to go?" she prompts.

Chase's eyes are staring at Parker.

"Chase?" She waves her hands.

He snaps back. "Huh?"

"Are you *listening*?"

"I was, I was. I'm just out of it."

Parker squeezes his hand. "I was saying that Jamie's having a little pool party on Sunday. It'll be fun. Twisted, no doubt, but fun. He's going to crank the heater so we can actually swim."

Chase shrugs, uncomfortable.

"Chase? What's wrong?"

"Nothing. I mean, I wouldn't mind just hanging on campus."

Parker puts her napkin on the table. "You *never* want to be on campus."

Chase fakes a laugh. "I don't know, Park. Lately, I just don't mind being on campus."

Parker smiles. "But Jamie's house will be more fun."

Chase clears his throat: "I just don't think you should be hanging with that dude."

Parker pauses. She registers what's been said. She grins, in an unkind way. "Jealous, much?"

Chase rolls his eyes. *So she's going to make this difficult, huh?* "Come *on*. I just think you might be getting ahead of yourself."

Parker's grin disappears. "How the hell am I getting ahead of myself?"

"You know, with the Oxy and all that shit. It's *shady*.

He's shady. He's nineteen, living at a pool house in the middle of nowhere, and handing out pills to pretty girls."

Parker licks her lips. Then she whispers, "I'm not going to raise my voice here, but don't you *dare* give me a lecture about partying."

Chase shakes his head in angry frustration. "It's not the same, what I do."

"Oh, really? How is it different, Chase? I'd love to hear this."

Chase grabs her hand but she pulls it loose. He sighs. "Maybe I am jealous, but I'm also worried about you. Oxy, I don't know. That stuff is different. And it just doesn't seem like, I don't know. . . ."

She watches him. *"What?"* she finally asks, in a biting way.

"It just doesn't seem like you're having fun sometimes."

"I'm capable of taking care of myself. Okay?"

Chase nods.

"You look like you don't believe me. How about this, Chase. Why don't you try stopping everything that *you* do, all the drinking and smoking and getting high and dipping. Go ahead. And then we can talk."

His head spins at the nastiness in her voice. He's never heard her like this.

They share cigarettes outside while waiting for the cab. They don't speak. He's staring at a lone horse hundreds of yards away. She may not have ridden away tonight, he thinks, but it won't be long.

Parker lights up a second smoke, eyes brimming. But she puts it out after one drag, and won't look at his inquisitive face. Guess now isn't the right time to talk to him about possibly being a father. She glances quickly at her belly, as if it might glow with life. Maybe she should buy her bus ticket now to get on *The Jerry Springer Show*: "Prep School Whore." She can see Chase slumped in one of the chairs onstage, having been wrangled there. Shaking his head, asking for a paternity test.

Parker can't think about what's happening in any logical way. She can only process it in grotesque rushes, in a stutter of images: a baby with no hands, a shotgun wedding, the medieval instruments at an abortion clinic—lined up and glistening on a tray.

18

That coquettish April sun is nowhere today, and Parker huddles next to a fire in Jamie's pool house while dark rain comes down. She's so not right. She denied it at dinner last week, but she knew it today when she lied about having to do work and then sneaking over here.

She *loves* the pool house, in a hateful way. The euphoria of being outside of herself. No pressure. All her tags are gone. She's not a financial-aid student. She's not from Canada. She's not a Rat. Not in love. Not potentially knocked up. She doesn't care. She's far away. She's nowhere.

Jamie slouches at the other end of the couch. They're alone. She blows bubbles with her gum as they watch *The Queen* on mute and listen to some Bristol dubstep too loud. Jamie pulls a prescription bottle from his shirt pocket. He hands an Oxy to Parker, who swallows it with a swig of warm soda. Jamie crushes his under an old NYU ID card. Parker watches him mash it into white powder. He fishes a cut straw from a drawer, does three lines, and leans back, holding his nose in quiet pain.

Parker's brain gets heavier and she lies down.

Jamie reaches for a smoke. "Sometimes I wonder why you come over here, Parker Cole."

Parker tries to open her eyes. She isn't sure why he's ruining everything by talking. "What do you mean?" she asks, her voice deep, slurry.

"Oh, luvvy. You can't bloody well pretend not to get my drift here."

Parker sits up, disheveled already. She looks at him, in his porkpie hat, white mesh shirt, and black jeans, dark circles under his eyes. She thinks of the day she met him at the gas station, and how cheerful he seemed. Buying lollipops, kicking snow in the lot. Driving like a hellion. She can't help it, she leans forward and puts her arms around his skinny torso, and he trembles to be held.

"Jamie, you're okay."

"I'm not okay," he says, his voice thick. "I gotta get out of here."

She rubs his arms, as if to warm him. She doesn't want him to leave Glendon, for many reasons, some of them selfish and unattractive. But there's a toxic air in the pool house. "Baby, have you thought that it might be time to go back to New York?"

She feels his head nod against her shoulder. "I have," he says, his voice muffled.

"Why can't you just get up and go?"

Jamie coughs. "I don't want to leave you."

Parker opens her eyes. Jamie kisses her. Parker lets him, and tastes his cigarettes, and desperation.

"I don't want you to leave, either," she says, but knows her motives are screwed up.

"And I got nowhere to go," Jamie says. "George, you know, the big man. He puts me up here. I'm supposed to be in school. I dropped out."

"You did?" she says, soothing him.

"But my parents, you know, they'd, like, kill me. George keeps my secret. He gives me money when I run out."

"Oh, Jamie," Parker says, and he reaches for her again.

That's all they do, kiss. When he starts to put a hand up her shirt, she moves away.

He pulls back to look at her, blurry-eyed. "You're with Chase, aren't you?"

Parker doesn't nod or shake her head. They watch each other.

"You can tell li'l ol' me," Jamie says, beaming suddenly.

"We're *kind* of together," she says uncertainly.

He yanks his arms from hers and stands up, walks over

to the bed with an unsteady gait, and flops down. She follows, sits on the edge. She rubs his back, but he flinches, like a dog who doesn't want to be touched. He turns his face away from her.

Parker watches Jamie for a while. Then she heads down the stairs, sits on the edge of his pool, whose tarp is off. The water is heavy when she puts her feet in, like fudge. It's heated up, as he promised.

She's cut in halves these days, and they meet at a membrane inside her. One part knows she's Parker. One part knows she's fucked. One part knows she's pregnant. One part knows she's not. One half believes there's a life growing in her belly, invincible. Or the miniature soul inside her is, at this very moment, getting twisted and tangled by chemicals.

Everything is insane.

Chase's eyes are glazed on the walk from the gymnasium. He slept for fourteen hours, then took Adderall for his third SAT attempt. He's inching toward respectability by Wellington standards, but the math kills. A tap on his shoulder.

"Hey, kid. What'd you think?" Nikki walks beside him.

Chase shrugs. "Eh. Who knows? I always think I could do better. What about you?"

Nikki laughs. "I hear you. I have no idea how I did. After looking at all those diagrams and sentence riddles and shit,

I barely know my name."

Chase shakes his head. "Can't wait to be done with it."

Nikki nods. "So how'd it go?"

He knows what she means. "Not so great, actually. She thought I was being jealous and said I was a hypocrite because of my partying. I just shut it down. I've barely seen her in the past few days."

"I saw her coming up from the woods yesterday. She looked like a zombie. Let me say something to her, 'kay?"

Chase nods. They look at each other; these are uncharted waters.

"She's going to get her ass kicked out at this rate," Nikki says.

"I know."

When Nikki gets back to Gray, her determination to talk to Parker is enhanced. Outside the dorm, she spots Parker walking Moses, who's crouched, shitting up a storm all over the lawn.

"What happened?" she calls to her roommate.

Parker turns a dismayed face to her. "Um. I fell asleep when he was in the room. He kind of ate the care package your dad sent. I'm so sorry," she says.

"Is he okay?"

Parker tries to smile. "Yeah, he will be. Nik, I'm really sorry."

When Nikki gets to the room, she's pissed. The

cellophane from the fresh-baked cookies is on the floor, torn, grimy with melted chocolate and dog spit. There're muddy paw prints on her bed. And chew marks on the heel of her Steve Madden boots. She looks at the mess for a minute, and then sets to cleaning it up. It's so not cool.

What happened to the butterscotch-ice-cream-loving, peppermint-tea-sipping, white-fur-coat-wearing, Dalai-Lama-quoting, Nick-Drake-singing, henna-tattooed, punk-rock, earnest, honest, nervous, nervy, lovely, lanky, tall girl from Canada with the cat-frame glasses? Where did Parker go?

Clichés pile up like old newspaper clippings. *One drug is the gateway to the next. Parker cares less about her life and more about her substances. She's changed. She's a stranger. She's at risk.*

It's a Stephen King movie. A good schoolgirl becomes inhabited by a space alien, and repeats all the cute sayings and knows all the personal details, but operates with marble eyes and a robot voice.

Wednesday lunch is sparse due to athletes traveling for away games. Parker has the afternoon off and feels sick. She isn't hungry but needs food. She grabs chicken nuggets—like the disfigured kind you get at Wendy's. They're bland enough, hopefully, to go down. She turns to leave with her folded paper plate of food.

Nikki stands before her with arms crossed. "Hey there."

"Hey." Parker can't quite look Nikki in the eyes.

"I have an idea. Why don't you join your old crew for an afternoon? We're going to Bridgeport to work on a park. Sound good? You have no play practice, right? Awesome, great."

"Yeah, but—"

"I never see you outside of our room anymore! This is fabulous." Nikki pulls a protesting Parker by the arm to the Woods Crew table.

"My God, Parker Cole," says Mr. Grant, the New Zealander and astronomy professor who leads Woods Crew. "I thought you left me for the theater."

"Just this spring, Mr. Grant, but I'll be back next year," Parker says, smiling.

"Parker is going with us to Bridgeport today." Nikki stares at Parker. "She has nothing to do so I recruited her."

Grant smiles. "Well done, Nicole. Shall we get on the road?"

Parker stuffs her head with her Walkman earphones on the ride there in the old junky Suburban. Fast-food signs and spring woods roar by. She smiles at Nikki once in a while to keep her off her back. Parker catches Grant looking at her—as if he's trying to remember how he knows her. It's not that, of course—but his face bears a message of effort. He wants to recognize her, and can't quite do it.

The Emerald Street Park is between housing projects in one of Bridgeport's dangerous neighborhoods. When they pull up, a crew of local kids watches with hands on hips. Grant introduces twelve Harding High School students who will be rebuilding the park with the Wellington group. The two groups unload dogwood saplings, their ends tied in burlap.

"Let's get to work, everyone. The main thing is giving the roots room—digging deep enough."

Nikki and Parker get attention from a few Harding boys.

"Whas good, prep girls?" a kid with two diamond studs says. His friends stand behind him. "I'm Jalil. This here is Tommy, Rocko, and Flip."

Nikki smiles. "First of all, I'm not preppy, so don't say that. Secondly, this is my friend Parker, and she is definitely not preppy either. And thirdly, can you guys give us a moment here?"

Jalil shrugs and backs away, smiling big. "Catch you later, sweet thing."

Nikki smiles. "Thanks, Jalil."

Parker is silent as she and Nikki sit on the curb.

"Park, why aren't you talking to me?"

Parker turns to face Nikki. "Um, what exactly should I be saying?"

"I'm worried about you. Hanging out with that townie."

"He's not a *townie*, and I haven't been hanging out with

him lately. I'm sick of getting lectures. You and Chase think you're somehow in a position to be telling me how to do things. Not really sure where you get off."

"I don't think we'd be lecturing you if you chilled out on the Oxy. You're acting like a junkie, babe. *Shouldn't* I be worried?"

"I'm fine, Nikki. Seriously, I just need some space. I have stuff to deal with."

"I told you about that girl Desi, from home. And they had an intervention."

Parker stands up and rolls her eyes. "Please. I have nothing to do with Desi from Long Island who had a *heroin* problem or whatever. Christ! Do you hear yourself?" Parker laughs bitterly, trying to sound lighthearted. "Come on, Nik! I party a tiny bit."

"I know, babe, it's just that—"

Parker's not listening. She's walking toward the shovels. "Let's go," she calls over her shoulder, without turning around.

They see Jalil standing over bulbs to be planted. Nikki smiles as Parker shakes her head. "Tattoos and earrings. I can't help it. It's the Long Island in me." Nikki tries to get her friend to crack but they work in silence.

This afternoon should be hopeful. The project is important—the vines will cover scarred and brutalized buildings, the trees will convert polluted air to clean oxygen, the green will bring back to life a dirty and mean landscape. But the guys from this area, popping gum and keeping their faces bland and benign as they dig, don't believe that the garden means much. It's an outsider's daydream, a good intention.

It's very possible that the bulbs won't sprout white roots in the earth. The leaves on the dogwoods are limp and sagging. They need sun and rain and luck to get sap running through their veins. Success largely depends on the weather in the next few days.

19

The first flower blooms on the Wellington campus: a tiny snowbell, in the shadow of Mr. Ballast's old bicycle which is leaned against the clapboard welding shed. The eastern meadow will soon be yellow with daffodil heads, octagons waving on stalks. The days are longer, the river rising. Spring is here.

Parker feels the swell. It amplifies her ups and downs. Her room is nasty; Nikki cleans up Parker's snacks. Parker's got plaque from forgetting to floss, she's lost weight, and she doesn't assemble her clothes with pleasure anymore. Her uniform is a tuxedo jacket over a floral dress and red boots. She wears it over and over. Sometimes, if she has a minute before the bell rings, she draws cat eyes.

She believes she's in charge. She's doctoring herself with the uppers–Ritalin and Adderall and whatever study drugs she scrounges. And then she's got a stash of downers from Jamie. The codes on the pills–numbers or symbols or letters stenciled by manufacturers–have become important hieroglyphics. Reminds her of the mood organ in her favorite sci-fi book, *Do Androids Dream of Electric Sheep?* She knows which button to press to feel better.

The fear of pregnancy she manages to deny, to delete. Almost.

The play is too soon. Parker crosses the wet green for her fitting. She's fidgety, her body at war with her. She's convinced Mrs. Jenkins will wind a tape measure around her waist and look up in horror: *You're pregnant!* Or she'll sniff Parker's chemical sweat and say: *Dear God, you're on drugs.* Mrs. Jenkins will kneel at Parker's hem and look up: *You're just a disappointment.*

Parker doesn't want to be touched.

"Hey, Juliet," Jorgen says.

"Hey, Romeo."

She enters the warren of dressing rooms. Passing an open door, she sees Miguel's torso. Photographs of past shows are pinned to bulletin boards, and the beehive hums with anxiety and old makeup and exhibitionism.

"Come on in, Parker," Mrs. Jenkins says, and waves her into a room where dresses hang from hooks on the wall.

Juliet's party dress is red velvet with gold stars. The lightbulbs around the mirror aren't bright, and the stars shiver dully. Next to it hangs the white nightgown, and a sleeping cap with crystals and ribbons. The black mourning dress hangs like a threat. Beneath each outfit are matching shoes, stitched with pearls or onyx.

"Wow, these are gorgeous," Parker says.

"Aren't they? They were created for a production in London, and we got them from there as one parcel. I think they date back to the 1940s, when everything was hand sewn."

"Can I try on the red dress first?"

Parker retreats to change in the bathroom. Takes off her boots and dress. She tunnels through the gown from the skirt up, reaching arms through the decades-old fabric, crinoline scratching her belly. She smells previous performances, the ghost of Juliets.

"What do you think?" she asks, coming out.

Mrs. Jenkins narrows her eyes. "Let's zip you up."

Parker holds her hair from the zipper. Then Mrs. Jenkins fixes the collar. She hands shoes to Parker.

"I think they're your size," Mrs. Jenkins says.

As Parker fits the golden slippers onto her feet, with their black nail polish and scarred heels, she feels like a ravaged Cinderella. But the shoe fits. Mrs. Jenkins scrutinizes her student. Her expression is the same one Parker's mom wore on Halloween. Genevieve would walk around Princess Leia or the flapper or Pocahontas, scowling, wondering what wasn't right.

Parker sweats. Her armpits reignite the old gown. Mrs. Jenkins pulls a thread off her sleeve. Parker's sure recognition has arrived. Mrs. Jenkins finally understands that she wasted attention and care on the wrong girl. Parker's hot, flushed.

"Hmmmm," Mrs. Jenkins says.

OhmyGod, I'm going to faint. Parker sees stars.

Mrs. Jenkins smiles. "You look beautiful."

Parker finds this unexpected and terrifying.

"Are you okay?" Mrs. Jenkins asks. "You're pink."

"Just warm. The dress, it's h-heavy," she stutters, and moves to the bathroom, where Juliet sits on the toilet and puts her face in her hands and tries not to sob out loud.

Why can't anyone see me? Parker thinks. *Come on. Take away my toys. Discipline me. Tell me I'm in trouble.* Meanwhile that's what her friends did, and she bit their heads off. Parker doesn't know what she wants.

Laine has the requirements for the May Day T-shirt, and knocks on Parker's door. There's no answer, so she opens the door to leave a note. But Parker's sitting right there. Her lamp is on, nothing else, so the room is dark. The bulb highlights her hair, her face. Parker lets out a croak, like a frog. Laine realizes she's bawling, and tries to disappear.

"What?" Parker says belligerently.

"I'm *so* sorry I just barged in."

Parker pushes hair back from her face, and swipes her finger under her eye to remove the black smudge. "What do you need?" she asks tearfully.

"Nothing," Laine says. "Nothing."

Parker's shoulders tremble, her chest heaving in her tank top. Laine feels an obligation to console. She moves forward, uncomfortable. When she kneels and puts her hand on Parker's arm, Parker cries harder. They sit like this, in the half-lit room. The window is cracked, and the spring night comes in, petal by petal.

"I just miss home," Parker manages to say at one point.

"I know," Laine says, soothing her. "I know."

Finally, Parker makes a sort of laugh. She shakes her head and smiles sadly. "Laine. I'm sorry. I'm a mess tonight."

"God, it's okay," Laine rushes to say.

"What's in the envelope?"

"Honestly, nothing urgent."

"Let me see."

"I'll leave it with you. You don't have to decide now if you want to do it."

Parker takes the package, wipes her cheeks again. "Cool," she says gruffly.

Laine does a funny thing; she tucks Parker's hair behind

her ear as she stands to leave. It's genuine affection. She means it.

"Listen," Parker says. "Don't tell anyone you caught me crying."

Laine promises.

That night Parker takes her last Oxy before bed. She wakes up at four A.M., sick, feverish. She pops half a Xanax and pours some of Nikki's Nyquil down her throat. She fears Nikki's eyes are glimmering in the dark, watching, but she might be paranoid. She's got Xanax and Vicodin. But for some reason, it's Oxy she craves. The next morning, she calls Jamie.

"Hey, kid! What's doing?" she asks in as jovial a tone as she can manage.

"Not a lot, dame," he says.

She waits for him to invite her over. "Well, take a wild guess what I need," she says, giving a world-weary and charming laugh. She's never heard herself talk like this.

More silence.

"God, I wish I never heard of the stuff!" she says in her new and horribly lighthearted tone.

"Listen, Parks. I can't bloody well keep handing you these things for free. Do you know what they cost?"

She *doesn't* know what they cost. "Tell me."

"Forty a pop, luv. Not bad, considering you're probably sharing with your mate Chase."

"A pill?" she asks incredulously.

"Yeah," he says.

"Forty a pill. Gotcha. See you later."

Parker marches down the green after class. It's sunny but she forgot her sunglasses so she squints. The Woods Crew kids squat in the garden, and the leaves are translucent. Piles of wilting weeds lie on the periphery. Tender tomato plants and string bean vines climb up stakes. Nikki stands and wipes her brow with the back of her wrist, as her fingers are muddy.

"Park," she says, confused.

Parker beckons her to the garden's edge. "Hey, doll. Any chance you could spare eighty bucks?"

"Why?"

Parker shrugs, sucking the tips of her hair.

"It's not like I wouldn't give it to you normally," Nikki says slowly.

Parker looks as if she'd just cursed her. "You're not saying what I think you're saying."

Nikki is uncertain. "I, uh. I'm just saying."

"I have *never* asked you for much," Parker says viciously, and her eyes fill with tears like rain in a clear sky.

"Okay, okay, jeez, Park. Don't freak out. It's in my underwear drawer; you know where it is."

Parker wipes her eyes, shakes her head. "I'm sorry, Nik," she says, almost laughing. "That was weird."

"Well, *shit*, dude," Nikki calls, like she's kidding. "Hey, babe, come on back," she tries, but Parker walks away.

When Parker gets to the pool house, having walked, Jamie's heading out for groceries. He's pale as the inside of a radish, and his hat is low over black sunglasses.

"Wow, didn't believe you'd make it here. Go ahead in, Miss Spontaneity. I'll be right back."

"Thanks!" she says as a cheerleader would.

Upstairs a skinny dude in overalls and no shirt is drawing in a kid's coloring book. Sage burns on a plate, the smoke twirling.

"I'm Keith," he says. "You're Parker."

She nods like he's as crazy as he is. "Correct." And then she looks for medicine. It's in Jamie's bedroom, in a cigarette case. She downs one. She puts another in her pocket, leaves the four twenties by the case. Dirty money. It grosses her out. She sits down on the couch, and watches Keith color Snow White's apron blue. Her body purrs. Waves of relief pass and she lets her eyes close. She doesn't dream.

When she wakes up, it takes time to understand what's happening. It's her feet. What's happening to her feet?

She manages to pry her lids open and look to the other end of the couch. Keith is rubbing her feet, and they're greasy with lotion. Her body is so sacked she can barely retrieve her limbs. Finally she tugs them away, like a body coming out of paralysis.

"What the hell are you doing?" she says fuzzily, wanting to kick him in the face.

"You didn't like it?" he asks.

She weaves to the door. She doesn't look back. Jamie's still gone, and she lopes down the drive, determined to get away from this place, and this drug, and herself.

She runs through the woods, where lilies of the valley are open in the shade. She doesn't see them. She's missed rehearsal. She doesn't care. The perfume of leaves and wild-flowers and oxygen don't reach her through the Oxy barrier. She runs.

She ends up in a very strange place.

In the front pew of the chapel. It's a nondenominational building, with no cross, no Torah. Just a steeple, an altar, a stone floor. She doesn't cry. She doesn't feel like crying. This emotion cuts her like a razor.

"What am I doing?" she asks the empty room.

It says nothing back. Which doesn't surprise her, as she's always loathed churches and religion and dogma and doctrines and rabbis and nuns and convents and prayers. But she can't get her eyes off that altar. It's pure and solid. Her life is dissolving, like Alka-Seltzer in a glass of water. What is there to hold?

She lies on the wooden bench and closes her eyes, her knees tucked up and one foot curled over the other, as if she were ten. It's so quiet she can hear panes creak. For the first time, Parker thinks about the afterlife. It's always been a cartoon notion, something born-again people believe because everything failed them in *this* life. They stand in circles in polyester suits and housewife dresses, their faces stress lined, and they daydream together. She swore she'd never buy into such bullshit.

But what *does* come next? Is this it?

An hour later, Parker pulls out of the daze. The room has darkened, the shadows dusty, the pews shining in the last light. She has made up her mind.

She steps up the stairs, and pauses. She fishes the pill out of her pocket and places it there, her divine offering. When she turns around, she beams.

In the dining hall, she eats minestrone, and it tastes good. She laughs with Mi-long and then eats lemon custard, drinks chamomile tea.

Two minutes before Check In, she races back to the chapel, with bile in her mouth, and trips up the steps. She gathers the pill into her hand, and thanks God it was still there.

20

Lupines bloom in the woods. Dandelions. Dogflower.

May Day arrives. A blue sky sizzles. Laine and Noah man the T-shirt booth. Laine pulls out an extra small for a Prep. Parker designed the shirt: a Mexican wrestling mask with *Día de Mayo* in script.

"Here you go." Laine smiles at the freshman. "What's your account number?"

"It's 11240. Jeanie Michaels. Thanks!"

"It'll look great on you," Noah says, and Laine hits his thigh under the table.

Laine looks good too, in her tee, Chaco sandals, and Patagonia shorts. The raffle tickets are going fast. Tiki didn't agree to a game with the winner, but Noah scored four box seats to a Giants home game. Trevor was impressed.

"All right, you two." Noah and Laine are startled by Caitlin's raspy voice. "Jimmy and I are here to relieve you of your duties. Great job."

"Yeah, go eat a funnel cake," Jimmy says. "Get a hot dog."

"Thanks, guys." Laine takes Noah's hand. "Shall we?"

Across the lawn by the Italian-ice stand is the dunking booth. Dean Talliworth, in khaki pants and a blue oxford, is climbing onto the plank. A line of students wait their turn. A couple of Upper-forms toss a football. The sun is gold and everywhere.

"Oh, I might have to get in on this," Noah says.

Behind the booth, Chase is toweling off. He only has on a pair of red Volcom board shorts. Parker's in torn jean shorts and a faded country-western button-down.

Parker's also in full-scale denial today. It almost makes her high to disregard reality. Last night she spent hours online looking up pregnancy signs and the reliability of early tests, but today she's pushed it all under the rug. Chase has become careful with her moods, terrified of pressing the wrong button, and so happy when she's happy, like today, that he doesn't push it.

"I mean, I got to throw, like, twenty times!" Parker is giving him shit about his short line. "You'd think you would have more enemies, Chase."

"You say this like you're disappointed, Park." Chase

drops the towel to the ground and slips on a gray American Apparel T-shirt and white flip-flops.

Parker wraps her arms around his skinny waist. "You look cute." She's been flirtatious. It might be the sugar in the air, or the fragrance of hot dogs and hamburgers. Or God knows what else.

"Hey, Parker," Laine shouts. It isn't until she and Noah round the corner that she realizes Parker isn't alone. "Oh, hey, Chase," she adds.

"Hi, Laine," Chase says.

"We didn't mean to interrupt," Laine says.

"No worries." Parker smiles.

"Just wanted to tell you, your shirts are a hit." Laine points at her own. "You like?"

"Looks good."

"Here, I brought you one. I knew white wasn't your color, so I had this one made, limited edition." Laine tosses her the black tee.

"Ha!" Parker unfolds the crumpled design. "How'd you know?"

"Wild guess." Laine smiles.

Before things get uncomfortable, Jorgen ambles by.

"Hey, Parker, some dude is asking for you," Jorgen says, wiping mustard from his chin as he eats a bratwurst. "In a hat. He's down by Lancaster."

"Shit," Chase murmurs.

"Who is it?" Noah asks Parker.

"Um, it might be my friend Jamie," she says uneasily.

Chase looks at Parker, who bites her nail.

"Is he . . . a townie?" Noah asks with attempted politeness.

"He's a *friend*, dude," Chase says. "Calm down."

"Chill out, you two," Parker warns.

"Yeah, please, come on." Laine stares at the guys, who look away.

"I'm just saying," Noah persists. "This is boarding school students only."

"How about I go talk to him?" Parker says, already moving away.

"I'll come with you," Chase says.

"Just get rid of him, Chase," Noah barks as Chase and Parker head down the hill.

"Relax, Noah," Chase says without looking back.

Parker and Chase find Jamie in the parking lot. He's sitting on the brick wall with Sophie.

"Hey, look-a-here, it's my girl and Mr. Chaz." Jamie hops down. "Where you been, kids?"

"Listen, Jamie, it's a private party today," Chase answers while walking toward them. "It's really lame and stupid, but you all are going to have to bolt."

"Actually, Parker invited us, so why don't you pipe

down." Jamie puts his hands on his hips and smiles like a skull.

Chase looks at Parker.

"Come on, you guys." Jamie holds his hand out for Parker's. "Let's go find those cabins you've been bragging about."

"Jamie, honestly," Chase says again. "I know it sounds stupid, but it's a closed event. I'm really sorry."

Jamie grins at Chase. "You *are* a sorry piece of ass, Chazzy. You really are."

Before Parker can say anything, Chase shoves Jamie, knocking him to the ground. He falls on top of him. In turn, Chase gets head-butted, and warmth oozes out of his nose. *Fuck.*

"Stop it!" Parker screams as Jamie gets up and kicks Chase in the stomach. "Just leave, okay? Please," Parker sobs.

"Fine. Whatever." Jamie cradles one hand in the other as he walks to his jeep. Sophie follows. "Just next time, think before you start mailing out invitations."

Chase lies still on the ground as Jamie drives off. He inventories himself before getting up gingerly. He spits a bright red puddle. Chase looks at Parker, who's crying, and then scans the scene. An empty parking lot.

"I'm so sorry, Chase," Parker says, keeping her distance.

At the infirmary, Chase invents a story about diving for

a ball in the volleyball tournament. He jokes about digging into a rock instead of a ball. The nurse doesn't laugh or ask questions while she plugs his nostrils. When he emerges into the waiting room, Parker's chewing her nails. Puffy eyes. Mascara running down her cheeks.

"Chase, I'm so sorry. Are you okay?"

"Well, I'm not going to *die*," Chase says quietly, trying to be funny.

"I didn't know he was going to show up."

"Really?" Chase asks, wincing as he touches his temple. "Didn't you invite him?"

"Well." Parker pauses. "I did. But I didn't think he'd show. I didn't."

"And what were you planning on doing, Park? Eat cotton candy and bob for apples all day? And if your drug dealer showed up, cool. Is that how you were going to handle it?"

"It's not like that, Chase. He's a *friend*."

"I wish that were the case, Park."

"I can't take this anymore," Parker says.

"Then don't," he says.

She stomps off, slinging her leather bag over her shoulder, glaring at him. Waiting for him to come get her, come chase her down, but he doesn't. She walks under the blooming apple tree, stumbles on a root, and keeps going.

* * *

Chase is out of the infirmary in time for the band. When he walks by the lit stage, Trevor is on the mike: "Please give a Wellington welcome to my favorite band, Jurassic Five!"

Enjoy it while it lasts, Trev. Next year you'll be cleaning puke in the Eating Club's basement. Chase shakes his head.

Noah and Laine clap with the May Day Committee on the side of the stage in a roped-off section. Chase catches Noah's eye. He'll deal with him later.

It's hard to make out the dark field. To afford J5, the committee sold tickets to nearby boarding schools. The number of ball caps and visors is staggering. Chase covers the lacrosse fields and finds Delia, Nikki, and Greg on a blanket near the back. Delia is leaning into Greg's chest. Nikki sits Indian-style, waving a glow stick.

"Hey, guys," Chase says. "Have you seen Parker?"

"Yo!" Greg points to Chase's nose. "I tried to come find your ass in the infirmary, but they wouldn't let me in."

"We heard what happened. We're so sorry," Delia says.

"Yeah, let's keep that between us, okay? No need for anyone to find out."

"I'm just sorry I wasn't there to drop that kid." Greg shadowboxes in slow motion.

"Sit down, Chase." Nikki pats the blanket. "Just take it easy right now."

"Has she gone to Jamie's, do you think?" Chase asks.

"Just sit down, man." Greg puts his arm around Chase.

"Here, have a chew and relax. Your face is screwed up, man. Just sit tight and we'll figure it out." Greg pulls a can of Copenhagen from his pocket.

Chase takes a deep breath.

Nikki looks at him. "What do you want to do?"

"I want to think for a minute," he says.

When Jurassic Five launches into "Work it Out," Chase lies on his back, eyes closed.

Don't stop stop your dreamin',
Let yourself float upon the notion
We can work it out, we gon' work it out, baby.

Chase gets up. He spits the wad of chew. "I'll be back, you guys."

They all look at him.

"We're coming with you," Greg says.

Chase shakes his head. "It's all good. I'll be back."

He walks to the trail through the woods, but a sense of urgency sends him jogging. Trees are thick with new leaves, and he runs among a blaze of forsythia. He's breathing hard, T-shirt soaked, and he turns his cap backward.

He emerges in Glendon on White Oak. He can smell it before he even gets up the drive, smoke drifting into the May sky. When he reaches the big house, it's a bizarre sight. The Bugatti is a black shell, burned and wet. A garden hose lies tangled on the lawn. The lilacs are scorched.

George is standing there, his face blotchy, his hair long

and wild. He's shirtless, and his gut hangs over pin-striped slacks.

"Get out of here," he growls with no preamble.

"What happened?" Chase asks.

"I'm not going to say it twice. Your friend was just here. I told her to scram too."

"We should call 911," Chase insists. "Your gas tank could be—"

"So help me God, if you don't get off this property, I *will* call 911. And tell them about all the nice little parties you kids had up there in the pool house."

Chase turns red. "Where's Jamie?"

Now George looks down, examining the ruined car again. "Fuck if I know. Hightailed it after this little number an hour ago."

Chase starts backing away from the man, from the scene. He looks at the brick house, the petals of lilacs black at the edges, the smoke coming from the carcass of the Bugatti. *Guess your boy had enough.*

What a melodrama. Jamie finally lashed out, and left. The beautiful machine is destroyed. Jamie had said that George loved that car, drove it all over New England—its leather seats were cracked and shiny, the glove box stuffed with maps, matchbooks from hotels, and mints from restaurants.

Jamie is an angry guy. He practices being happy—loving

others, trusting others. And when he fails, he breaks their toys. Chase thinks that he's gone now from George's life, and from Parker's. Jamie's the sort to vanish and never return. Chase finally sees how badly Jamie did want to connect, by way of his vicious disappointment when it fell through. Jamie will move into someone else's pool house soon. He'll build another palace of cards designed to fall down.

Parker, after seeing the car herself, came back to Gray. She's in the shower, shaking.

She keeps thinking about that gas station girl with the lavender eye shadow. The one who couldn't smile, not if a gun were to her head. Was she a dropout? A bad mother or a good mother? She couldn't be more than seventeen. Did her own mom take care of her baby while she checked out customers, ringing up their gas, their cigarettes, their sodas, their candy? Did her mom chain-smoke and watch soap operas, and then fetch her daughter at twilight, driving a ruby Oldsmobile through snow?

Parker turns off the water and folds a towel around her body. She realizes she thinks about that girl every day. She even remembers the orange hooded sweatshirt she wore, pilled from washings.

Last year, Parker somehow escaped being a contender in the Crash Test Bet. She wasn't profiled in the hate book. Nikki seemed the one to put your money on, as she flagrantly tried and failed to be a part of Wellington. But it was Laine who got drop-kicked in the end, stumbling around a hotel roof in the snow, high on coke, barefoot in a party dress.

Parker thought the bet was over. Now she thinks she's wrong. It goes on and on. It wasn't Schuyler who designed it; the architecture is bigger than that. Teen girls all over the world race neck and neck—to abortions, to Oxy, to anorexia. Or to summa cum laude or hot boyfriends or tennis trophies. Or to love and peace of heart and integrity. They are all tested. Parker wonders if they all get to where they're going by a conspiracy of outside forces, or by free will. Parker wonders if the gas station girl ever feels like a mannequin flying through the broken windshield of a car.

Later that night, Chase digs around his desk for a number. He finds it in his old limnology notebook and breathes deeply before dialing. He's not sure what he's going to say. A deep voice picks up.

"Hello?"

"Hello. Mr. Cole?" Chase recognizes the voice from his trip north last summer.

"Ye-s-s-s?"

"This is Chase Dobbs. Parker's friend."

"Sure. How are you, Chase?"

"I'm fine, Mr. Cole." *Should I be doing this?*

"Well, what can I do for you, Chase?"

Chase's hands grow clammy. He tastes the salt on his bottom lip. *This isn't right. I'm not a narc.* "Well, Mr. Cole, I just wanted to tell you that Parker has a big performance in the school play coming up, and I'm not sure if she told you, but it would mean a lot if you came down to see it."

"She did tell me about that. Unfortunately, I don't think we'll be able to make it with exams and all up here, but I appreciate you calling." Mr. Cole sounds uncertain. "Are you sure there's nothing else?"

"Nope, nope. That's it. Talk to you later." Chase hangs up before saying good-bye.

This is the first time Chase feels that he is failing himself. It used to be that he was failing his dad, or the school, or some expectation the world had of him with which he didn't agree. He needs to help Parker. But he doesn't want to get her kicked out. What are the rules for this? He sits in his room, and he doodles stars and moons over his notebook. He draws Orion.

Parker is *here*, but when Chase reaches out, his arms pass through her, like a finger through a candle flame.

His mind wanders to even darker matters. All year people have gossiped about the suicides. How one guy at Northfield Mount Hermon jumped off the Humanities Building and landed on a lawn mower, breaking himself. A girl at Kent checked into a small-town motel and sliced her wrists with a razor blade, passsed into the next life while lying in

232

a grimy tub. What letters they left have been resealed, like classified documents.

And Chase is obsessed with these notes. He wonders how someone could use a ballpoint pen and a sheet of paper to make that profound good-bye. He pictures pages covered in script, an exotic language of anger and resentment and fear and departure. Are they like thank-you cards, grateful to the hosts for showing them a good time while it lasted? Or Dear John missives, talking about how love doesn't always last? Chase can't conceive of a poem, and he has trouble even beginning essays. How on earth do you write the end?

21

Dusky moon. Parker hurries to the auditorium. She woke up to blood in her underwear this morning, and ever since she's been high and dazed. There is no future inside herself.

A gypsy scarf is wrapped around her neck, coins jangling from its fringe. She's wrecked with stage fright. This is worse than what she feared. Her nerves are like the ends of the copper wire you plug into speakers: bundles of prickly threads. Mist lies on the lawn, and her Adidas sneakers are soaked.

"Break that leg, Park!" says Jackson as they cross paths.

She gives him a wry smile. "Thanks."

When she enters dressing rooms, Mrs. Jenkins has bobby pins in her mouth and is answering questions from half-clothed actors. When she sees Parker, she takes the pins out.

"Parker! You're a half hour late! What on earth? Hop into your dress; let's go," she says sternly.

"Sorry," Parker says.

Makeup is a chaos of colors and brushes. Girdles and shoes and breeches hang from hooks or lie across tables, unzipped and split, showing their unglamorous insides. Parker stands in the corner and breaks an Oxy in half, then breaks an Adderall in half, and slugs them both with someone's Arizona iced tea, warm and stale.

"Hey!"

Parker whips around, and Jorgen is leaning into the threshold. "H-hi," she stutters guiltily.

"You're going to do great, Juliet," he says.

"Thanks," she says, and only later will she wonder why she wasn't polite enough to say he would be great too.

The cast is readied in a flurry of ribbon-tying and foundation-smearing, and the curtains swish open, stagehands hanging on cables. From the wings, Parker sees what an audience looks like, their heads indecipherable as eggs in a carton. There is an amber glow, the darkness caught in the crevices between seats.

She gulps.

Ted Westerville, the narrator, is alone onstage, blanched in a royal-blue coat, the ruffles of his cuff like foam as he gestures: "'But passion lends them power, time means, to meet/ Tempering extremities with extreme sweet.'"

The Oxy satisfies need; the Adderall tempers its slushiness. Her heart is a bongo drum. This is a dream she's watching, isn't it? Okay, now she feels stronger.

I've got to get through this performance, she thinks. *I can do this. Step by step, I'll walk across the stage and then go home to sleep. Tomorrow I will figure out this mess. Tomorrow I will start over. I will ask for help.*

The curtain closes; the stage is set by stagehands. Parker watches the curtain open.

She's up.

Scene three. Parker stands on the stage in a nightgown with the Nurse and Lady Capulet. Luckily, Juliet is barely included in the initial dialogue. Juliet's mom tells her she must marry Paris.

Parker says her first line clear as a bell, distilled by chemicals: "'How now! Who calls?'"

The scene continues, and Parker glows. Maybe she'll be great. The Oxy is working. The curtain slams, and Parker is patted on the back as she glides off. Her pulse is banging.

Backstage, everyone is sweating, costumes getting oily, faces shining. Parker's aware her perception is off, but she feels good. *It's just one hour,* she thinks. *An hour. One hour.*

Onstage, she talks with Romeo, realizes he's the son of her family's enemies. She says to the Nurse: "'My grave is like to be my wedding bed.'" It's then she glimpses Chase; her eyes have been scanning the audience.

She stumbles over her next line: "'My only love sprung from my only hate!'"

When she makes it backstage she wipes her forehead. It's wet. Sarah Eller eyes her.

"You doing okay?" Sarah asks.

"Yeah, fine," Parker says.

Never before has Parker talked so sternly to herself. *You pull it together, RIGHT NOW. I will NOT forgive you if you don't get through this. Focus.*

She goes back out. She sees roses, the shimmer of cellophane in Chase's lap. She knows he's rooting for her. And she makes it through the next acts. Tybalt, who belongs to Juliet's family, kills Romeo's best friend, Mercutio. Romeo sees red and slaughters Tybalt, then realizes what he's done, and hides in the friar's cell. Romeo is banished, and hangs out with Juliet for one night before skipping town. The two are in love.

Parker marches in and out of lines, on- and offstage, lets herself be buttoned and rouged. She forgets not one line. But she feels it, between acts three and four. She's coming down. She takes the second half of Oxy. *Home stretch.*

This is the red velvet dress scene.

She looks dazzling, Chase thinks. *She seemed nervous but she got into it. Her voice is lush, like when she's high, but maybe that's just from being onstage.* He looks at people in his row; everyone is attentive.

Juliet takes poison to sleep in this scene. But everyone will think she's dead. They'll put her in a tomb, where she'll wake next to Romeo, and they can be together.

In her opening lines, Parker stutters. Chase mouths the words, as he practiced lines with her. The mother tells Juliet, "Get thee to sleep." Then she and the Nurse leave the room, and Juliet is alone.

Chase fidgets. *Come on, Park. Come on, babe.*

Parker looks out, face chiseled by lights. Her arms stark in the gown. Chase can see diamonds of sweat. She holds out her hands, palms up.

"'I have a faint cold fear thrills through my veins,'" she says.

She's doing the monologue too slow. Chase taps his foot.

"'My dismal scene I needs must act alone,'" she says, skipping lines.

Shit, Chase thinks. He wonders if everyone can tell she's dropping lines.

"'What if it be a poison?'" she asks, confused.

A spectator coughs, another clears his throat, and Parker looks into the dark.

"'Shall I not, then, be stifled in the vault?'"

Mrs. Jenkins hovers in the wings. There's muttering in

the audience. Chase stares at Parker.

"'O, if I wake, shall I not be distraught?'" she asks, distraught.

Get her off the stage, Chase thinks. *Please.*

As she staggers now, like an old bum in the street, people half stand in their seats, and there's hushed talking.

Parker's on hands and knees. "Romeo?"

The curtain yanks shut, and teachers run-walk backstage.

As Parker fell down, she hallucinated her father in the audience—his narrow face and braid, the earring, his corduroy jacket.

The lights are up onstage, the magic extinguished. Parker's eyes are rolled back. Mr. Hartigan holds an ammonia-soaked paper towel under her nose. And here comes Parker's dad, through the curtains, in the flesh. When she wakes up, he's the one sitting cross-legged on the floor, which is tape-marked for props and actors, her head on his knee. He's the one who cradles her.

"You're okay, pumpkin. I'm here. I'm here."

The teachers give them room, stand with arms crossed. *Nerves,* they murmur to one another. But Gary isn't listening. He's looking at his daughter's face, and trying not to cry. His baby is not okay. He can feel it pass from her skin to his, like electricity.

22

Gary tells Chase to call him by his first name. They're in Gary's rented Kia, with Parker drowsing in the backseat. The town is dead, and they drive without further conversation. At the edge of Glendon are gas stations, an auto body shop, a TGIF and Gary's Super 8 motel. They pull up.

Chase has been allowed here by Mr. Ballast, who at first, when Gary asked for Chase's help, said no. Chase had to be in his room by Check In. Gary looked at Mr. Ballast a beat before he repeated himself. Chase had never seen anything like it. The man didn't raise his voice. His earring trembled as he waited for the right answer.

"Come in," Gary says now, and Chase hurries to obey.

Gary guides Parker into the room and strips off the spread, pulls down sheets. While she sits, head bowed, her father kneels to untie her shoes. Chase is terrified. He looks at the mirror between beds, the remote control on the bedside table, Gary's luggage on a chair, untouched. He must have come in just to drop off his things and then gone straight to the theater.

"Okay, pumpkin," Gary says now, and Parker tips over to be tucked in.

He stands and looks at her; she's breathing raggedly and her brow is furrowed, but she's asleep. He then looks at Chase. Chase has never felt so small.

"Come out here." Gary beckons.

They walk out the back door to a dry patio. A light full of dead insects hangs on the wall. Gary pulls plastic chairs to their doorstep, and they sit. He bumps a pack of Winstons out of his jacket pocket and then holds it between his teeth as he takes the jacket off, throwing it over the arm of his chair as if he were angry with it. He slips a lighter from inside the pack, and he's smoking.

"What's going on?" he says evenly, but he doesn't mean it casually.

Chase is sweating like an animal. "I don't know what to tell you, sir," he starts.

"Think," Gary says, and exhales.

Chase's mind whirls. How to get Parker help without getting her in trouble? How can he turn her in? How could he do this, and look himself in the mirror?

"I mean, she's been acting strange; I think the pressure of school and stuff is taking a toll," he begins.

"She's high as a fucking kite, Chase," Gary spits out.

Chase now stares at the man.

Finally Gary sighs, stubs out his cigarette, lights another one. He looks at Chase for a long time. "Let me begin again. Because you and I don't know each other. I think I'm coming off the wrong way. I'm upset, Chase. My daughter is a mess. This is scary. You understand? I'm not mad at you. Or anyone. I want to make her better; I need to help her. You need to tell me the truth."

"Got it," Chase says, nodding fast.

"What's she on?"

Chase swallows hard, but this is his last hesitation. "Oxy-Contin. Adderall. I don't know what else; I honestly don't. And I don't know how much, but . . ."

"But you think it's a lot."

Chase looks at the sky, dirty clouds against black night. "I thought I noticed in her these patterns, like, I never saw them in anyone else. If she didn't have something in her system, lately, it seemed that she was . . . getting sick, I guess." Chase sinks. These are horrible words to say to a father.

Gary's nodding. "Sick."

"God, I'm sorry. I'm sorry this happened. The only thing I can say, though, is the school has no idea. No one knows."

Gary scoffs at that. "I wish they *had* known. I wish they paid attention to her."

Chase looks at his shoes, ashamed of having said the wrong thing.

"How'd she get the stuff?"

"This guy Jamie, who lived in town. I knew he was a bad friend. This happened pretty much overnight, you know? I honestly didn't think this could happen so fast."

Gary snorts. "Sure it can."

They sit for a while. The lights go off behind the curtains of another room, the fabric losing its red glow. Somewhere, like invisible dinosaurs, trucks groan, switching gears.

Gary sends his cigarette stub in an arc by flicking it. He clasps his hands together. "This is my fault."

He and Chase look at each other. Chase is speechless.

"I handed her down some of the worst DNA you ever heard of. When it comes to addiction, I've been down every dark road. I know where that girl is right now. That's why this is killing me."

They sit for a few more moments.

Gary lights up again. "Sorry, my last vice." He exhales. "Genevieve, you know, Parker's mom, and I argued about it a lot. Whether to tell Parker or not that she might be a time bomb. I didn't want her to go through life thinking she was flawed, or believing she might have all these huge problems—when there was no way of knowing, really, if she *did* inherit that predisposition. Genevieve was right. We should have told her. This wasn't fair."

"What can I do?" Chase says.

Gary looks at him. "You've done a lot by talking with me here. I appreciate it, Chase." He grabs Chase's shoulder. His grip is powerful; his hands are huge and spidery. "Now I have to take her home."

"What are you going to tell the school?" Chase says fearfully.

Gary looks at him like Chase is slightly mad. "I could not possibly care less about the school."

They enter the room, and Parker is fitful. Gary calls a Glendon cab service for Chase. They shake hands. There's so much Chase wants to ask, but boiled down it comes to this: *When can I have her back?*

At five A.M., Gary gets Parker out of bed. He wipes her face with a towel. Father and daughter sit on the bed in the motel room, looking into each other's brown eyes. The sun won't rise for another hour. The lot outside is quiet, glittering with glass.

"Do you want to go get some stuff from your room?" he asks very softly.

She nods.

They steal up to Gray, which is silent. They're like thieves on its stone steps. Gary stands in the lit hall while Parker rummages around the dark room. She doesn't wake Nikki, who will always be angry Parker didn't say good-bye. Parker takes very few things.

When she emerges, and closes the door stealthily behind her, Gary is amazed at how well she's doing. Now he needs to get her to the airport.

They go down the stairs and load her bag into the car.

"Dad, I forgot something," Parker says. "I've got to run up to my room."

He looks at her. Her face is lean and sad, but honest, he believes. He's worried, because she's at the point where addicts get squirrelly. But he lets her go. She steps into the building, carefully closing the door.

He leans against the car, and is looking at the stars when he hears a noise. Lights click on in the apartment on the first floor. A dog barks. He starts running.

In the foyer, Parker is on her knees, pulling at the collar of a dog, and a woman in her robe is talking sternly to Parker.

"I'm taking him," Parker cries.

Mrs. Jenkins shakes her head. "Parker, where?" She looks up and sees Gary.

"I'm Parker's dad," he says grimly, and he approaches his daughter, who turns a desperate face to him.

"Moses has to come," Parker says.

"Moses can't come," he says. "He can't come on the plane, Parker."

"He has to!" she shrieks.

Doors start opening along the floor, girls' faces peeking out.

Mrs. Jenkins looks sadly at Gary to handle this. He kneels by Parker with all the calmness and patience he has in him. He pries her fingers from the collar. Moses looks on with terror, his body balking.

"No," Parker cries, folding onto the floor once the dog is released.

Moses doesn't retreat into the apartment, but stands there, staring at Parker, bewildered, whimpering. Gary takes his daughter into his arms, there on the floor, and he cranes his head around to mouth to Mrs. Jenkins that she should shut the door. She nods and pulls Moses with her.

Gary picks up Parker, as if she were five again, and carries her to the car. Doors shut one by one as they pass, and girls run to their windows to see Gary put her in the passenger seat, turn on the headlights, and leave.

Gary and Parker are on the plane at eight A.M. She's white as paint, and shivering. He's stoic, miserable, willing to trade places with her in a heartbeat. He holds her hand as the plane takes off. Parker can't bear to look out the window as

246

Connecticut—with its dandelions and lilacs and dogwoods and tulips—disappears. She tries to make herself, but she can't. *I'm so sorry,* she whispers.

Chase waits all the next day for a call. No one knows anything. The scene from Gray gets broadcast around campus immediately. The dog, the crying, the Kia driving through the gates. He goes through classes like a sleepwalker. It's a beautiful day, the air bright with cut lawn. He walks through the main building, whose windows are open. Past antique lamps with pleated silk shades, and teachers' offices dense with plants, books, papers, and coffee mugs. He walks through the music wing, the stands holding sheet music like prayer books.

"Chase, what's up?" asks Kelly Genner, an Upper-form, and Chase walks right by her.

He lands in his room and sits at his desk, looking at nothing. Lately he's been thinking about this kid from Charleston. His nickname was Raz; Chase doesn't know his real name. His older brother had died in a car wreck after drinking and shooting speed or something. Raz looked like a skinhead, but he was all about clean living and tolerance. He wore T-shirts that said *Drug-free,* and had a tattoo of a dove on the inside of his forearm.

Chase and his buddies made relentless fun of him.

Chase wonders where Raz is right now.

He gets the call around eight P.M.

"Is this Chase?" a woman asks.

"Yes, ma'am," he says, nervous and formal.

"It's Genevieve. Parker's mom."

"How are you, ma'am?"

"I've been better," she says, almost giving a husky laugh. She sounds exhausted. "Parker wanted you to know that she's here, with us, and that she's okay."

"Oh, all right," he says.

"And *I* wanted to say, thanks for talking to Gary and everything. You made a difference."

"You're welcome, of course," he rushes to answer. "Is she, uh . . . I guess she's probably not making it back to finish the semester or anything."

There's a brief silence, and Chase knows everything in that one moment. He doesn't need Genevieve to tell him that Parker will never be coming back. But she tells him anyway.

"I'm so sorry, Chase," she says.

"Right," he says. "Me too."

He sits there for another stunned hour or more. Processing, processing. At nine thirty, a knock.

Noah puts his curly-black-haired head in the door. He steps in, his checkered Vans muddy from the walk over here. His hands are sunk into his gray linen pants, and he walks over to his friend.

Chase stands up and Noah hugs him, like family. Chase won't let himself cry; that's insane. But they stand there, and Noah pats him hard on the back.

"Dude," Noah says eventually, but that's all.

Jimmy from the first floor knocks on the door. "Hey, Chase. A girl's downstairs."

Noah and Chase stomp down the marble steps and meet Nikki in the foyer. Her eyes are red and swollen. They all hug.

Nikki holds up a black shirt. "I brought this for you," she says, handing the Ramones T-shirt to Chase.

He smiles bittersweetly. "How will she survive without this?"

"Should we have done something more?" Nikki asks worriedly.

Chase shrugs. "Yeah. I think so. I think we should have done a lot more."

"You guys shouldn't be down on yourselves, though," Noah says. "It's not like we've been through this already. No one knew what to do."

They stand there, thinking about this, in the high-ceilinged foyer, the radiators all shut off, cold to the touch. Guys start slamming through the big front door, on their way back from the snack bar, talking and whistling and knocking one another around as they return for Check In.

"What makes me crazy is that this will just get swept

under the rug," Nikki says. "She's just going to be gossip; she's not coming back."

Chase looks away, tears biting now at his eyes.

Noah takes the shirt from him. "I have an idea."

They walk together to the main circle, where the flagpole is. The dorms are lit up, everyone back in their rooms. It's two minutes to Check In. Noah unlaces the line from the pole, and lowers it. He attaches the T-shirt by its sleeves, raises it.

Chase almost laughs with sadness and giddiness. "Are we crazy?"

Noah grins. "I don't know. This might be retarded; I have no idea. But we're going to remember Parker tonight."

Nikki stands with hands on hips, and eyes glazed from crying, and watches the shirt get hoisted.

It flies, the white lettering bright against the sky. Noah cleats the rope, and the three of them stand there and look at the pennant. They've missed Check In.

"This is like a scene from a bad boarding-school movie," Chase says under his breath, and they all laugh.

"I know," Nikki says. "It's like the finale of *Seinfeld* or some shit."

For some reason, the school allows curfew to be broken. The friends stand there for a while, daring anyone to tell them to take it down. They shiver. They're thinking of games and pranks, autumn fields and spring waterfalls, of getting drunk on smuggled-in bourbon or chain-smoking Camels, of kissing and crying, of dancing at formals, and sleeping through classes. They're remembering Costa Rica and Manhattan, going AWOL to Pawling, Charleston, limousines and surfboards, white lies and heavy petting, bad days and good nights.

Good friends can give friendship a hard ride. They test it. They want to see how far the machine will go, and how fast. But not everyone will survive a crash.

23

ven with shades drawn, Chase senses the chaos. Hours earlier he was woken up by guitar riffs from Slash and beats from 50 Cent. Then Gucci loafers and driving shoes sound through the hall. Occasionally he hears a roar as the animals prepare for emancipation. *Fucking graduation day.*

In the movies, graduation means bawling students, a bear hug between jock and tutor, the misty-eyed bon voyage a teacher gives to her pet. Chase doesn't care about melodrama today. Not that kind, at least. All he hears are the car horns of overpacked Range Rovers, and the jeers and whistles as seniors piss on the front steps of their dorms, writing their good-byes in script.

What really gets Chase are the exchanges between boarding-school renegades and their French-cuff fathers.

That moment when a strong handshake morphs into a man-hug. When the old fellow removes his reading glasses and dabs his eyes with a Brooks Brothers pocket square. It reminds Chase of commercials about putting money away for your kid's college fund.

Chase covers his face with his pillow. By noon, graduates (with cool parents) will be swilling champagne and smoking cigarettes at local restaurants. Then they'll ride into the sunset, toward a chain of graduation parties, caravanning down the East Coast, from estate to beach house to penthouse. Puking and smoking, falling in love and almost getting arrested, driving and crying, and ultimately finding their way home, where they'll sleep off the memories.

Chase gets up. Sits at his desk surrounded by loose-leaf notes for his almost overdue philosophy paper on Socrates. None of this wisdom makes sense right now.

Even though Chase hates smoking in the morning, he has to calm his nerves. He misses Parker so much he's shaking. How can he make it through this? She's already a boarding-school folktale. He's sure kids at Cate in California or Madeira in Virginia have heard the sad story about Parker Cole, that girl at Wellington, the one with the top hat and leopard pants, who liked the Cure and Norwegian death metal, the painter, the girl who fell down onstage, the *addict*.

The door opens without a knock. Chase turns to Greg,

and then he takes a drag on the cigarette burning between his two fingers.

"You might want to use this, kid." Greg reaches around Chase to snap on the fan.

"Thanks," Chase says, coughing.

Greg sits on the bed and surveys the room.

"So, things aren't so good, huh?"

Chase snorts in reply.

"It wasn't your fault, Chase."

"It's not even that." He puts out his cigarette. "*Maybe* I could have helped her. All that matters is she's gone."

Greg sits watching his best friend. Then he takes the pack of Parliaments from Chase, and crumples it in one hand. Drops it in the garbage.

Noah shifts gears in a 1985 red Mercedes convertible borrowed from his uncle as he and Laine inch down Route 27. It's the first week of June, and the Hamptons have not yet been invaded by the renters, clubbers, and pastel gangs. Laine's wrapped in a camel-beige cardigan Noah calls her "burrito." Top's down.

Tory Lundress was only slightly popular at Wellington, though she traveled in the right circles. Her claim to fame is a Sagaponack beach house. The 12,000-square-foot mansion houses her mother and thirteen-year-old sister and a staff of eight. Her father moved to Palm Beach with his life partner, Sven, five years earlier. Tory's family makes for good gossip.

The Lundresses' driveway is already littered with beer bottles. Laine and Noah give each other a look: *Here goes.*

This is the last night of senior parties. A weeklong bender has taken the group from Milford, New York, to Westport, Connecticut, to Chatham, Massachusetts, to Martha's Vineyard to Newport and finally to Sagaponack.

Noah and Laine get out of the car and stretch, stand together and stare at the house. Both are nervous about what type of party awaits. The party the night before, at Caitlin's grandmother's estate in Newport, was over the top. Twenty kegs, enough liquor to incapacitate al-Qaeda, two bands, a rave, and a drum circle that awoke roosters.

Noah's worried too, because rumors are flying that Collin O'Mara and Jeff MacArthur, the expelled lacrosse PGs, are showing up for payback. And Noah knows Chase is on his way here to catch the last party. This could be a problem.

Last night, Noah passed out in a freakin' *horse* stall and has been picking straw out of his clothes all day. His memories are blurry. Jell-O shots, keg stands, a nitrous balloon, a bet with Gabriel about who could ride a horse, taking a leak in an empty stall, blackness. He apologized a thousand times to Laine, whom he found curled in the backseat of the Mercedes this morning. *It's cute,* she told him. *We both have a thing for horses.*

Through the window of the foyer, Noah can tell the party's in full swing. Tents are assembled on the back lawn just yards from the Atlantic Ocean. Cooks man barbecue stations, bartenders overserve, and a cluster of forty-something women chaperone, champagne glasses held in their bejeweled and tan hands.

Noah gets a Heineken and stands by a heated game of Beer Pong. A slap on the back startles him. He turns to see O'Mara and MacArthur. Both are wearing corduroy jeans and have beards, and their eyes glitter.

"I heard you made All New England, superstar."

Noah nods, half choking on his beer.

MacArthur pats him on the head. "Don't be so modest, ace. I'm glad you got your shot."

Noah tries to smile. "Thanks, man. I just felt bad, you know."

O'Mara laughs. "What? Because we got tossed and didn't get into Princeton and UVA like originally planned?"

"Yeah, I guess," Noah replies.

MacArthur shakes his head. "You 'guess,' that's funny. So, where's your boy Dobbs? You seen him?"

"I have no idea. I just got here."

O'Mara gives Noah a pat on the shoulder. "Could you

tell that chickenshit we're looking forward to catching up with him?"

"Actually . . ." Noah brushes off O'Mara's arm. His face breaks into an angry sweat. "About Chase. Since I invited him to Florida, if you *really* believe he got you busted or whatever, I was thinking maybe I should get some blame. Though you're both dumber than you look if you think it was anyone's fault but your own."

O'Mara's and MacArthur's eyes widen. They look over Noah's shoulders at the chaperones gyrating to Devo's "Whip It." O'Mara looks at MacArthur and smiles. "We'll catch up with you later on too, Mr. All New England."

Noah stands alone, sun beating on his face.

Laine sits with friends. She overhears murmurs about Parker Cole. Some say it was coke, others heroin. She spots Noah across the lawn. Their eyes meet and they share a smile: *Thank God I have you.*

That evening Chase finds Noah and Laine on one of the main house's decks overlooking the beach. Laine is leaning into Noah, who looks relaxed with his arms wrapped around her olive Patagonia vest. Chase smiles and politely asks Laine if he can have a word with her boyfriend. Laine looks up at Noah, who says that he'll come find her in a sec.

"How is she?" Laine asks as she gets up.

"Not sure," Chase says.

When the guys are alone, Chase breaks it down.

"Dude, I heard about what you said to O'Mara and MacArthur."

Noah remains quiet, unsure where this is headed.

"You know," Chase continues, "most likely, we'll both get our asses kicked now, and you *probably* don't even deserve it." Chase laughs.

Noah squints at his friend, the surf pounding the dark beach. A memory comes back from his first day at Wellington, when he and Chase walked down Dory Hill to the orientation picnic at the lake. If he'd been solo, he would have been shitting bricks. Chase had his back. Chase treated him like a confidant that day, always choosing him to mutter his brutally funny and keen oberservations to. They sat at a table and ate, and Chase introduced Noah to everyone they met. The lake radiated blue behind them, and their future unfolded in front of them. They ate grilled chicken and sipped lemonade, and Noah thought that maybe he could survive boarding school. Maybe he would even have a good time.

But somehow getting slipped under Chase's wing also meant he was second to Chase. This year, he's grown out of that, and Chase hasn't liked it. So they battled. It was a struggle that couldn't be hurried or interrupted, and the spectators watched with dim eyes and crossed arms. The two friends wrestled, locked, angry.

Now they're tired—and willing to acknowledge each other's strength. Time to release. They're suddenly and finally equals.

"Maybe I deserve it a little bit, you know?" Noah smiles.

"I'm sorry, man." Chase holds out his hand. They shake under the Milky Way of stars.

The second week of outpatient rehab isn't better than the first. Looking around the sterile room, Parker feels more out of place than at Wellington. Grackles fight outside the window. The group members saunter in, pour coffee from the machine into their paper cups.

"How you all doing?" Kylie, the leader, asks, as she enters with her clipboard.

The chemical need is out of Parker's system; at first she was sick, sicker than she's ever been. But now she needs to deal with a permanent desire triggered in her heart and mind. She's acquainted with a euphoria that she'll always want.

The group sits in a circle, which forces eye contact and interaction. Out of the eight patients, five are here for meth and two for heroin, which makes Parker the Oxy oddball. The meth-heads are first-time offenders, here as part of a sentence. The heroin addicts are a married couple forced by the courts to give up their three-year-old girl and get treatment. They've been cursing at each other. Parker has learned more about these strangers than she wants to know.

Kylie, the heavyset therapist, in dark jeans and a sweatshirt with two black Labs on the front, is irreverent and hoarse. *I am somebody* and *Fake it till you make it* and *Easy does it* are written on the board in pink chalk.

Adrianne, a meth user, is twenty-five. Parker can't believe she's that young. She has a scab on her chin. Adrianne is bawling about how her uncle used to make her take baths with him until she was thirteen. Parker can't help but think, when she hears these stories, that Parker herself had no right to fall apart. Kylie tells her that it's not that simple.

The Subaru Outback is waiting after the meeting. Finn's in the backseat, backpack on his lap. Parker opens the passenger door. She doesn't feel like getting into it with Finn again. Despite her objection, her parents chose to be honest with him: "Parker is sick. She has a problem with a drug called Oxycodone. We need to take care of your sister until this problem goes away."

But no matter how they explain it, Finn's questions keep coming back to the same issue: the *why* part. Parker knows he's too young and naive to understand.

"So, how did it go today?" Genevieve looks at her daughter.

"It's kind of torture," Parker says, looking at the anti-quated facility as they drive away. "I hope I'm not like them," she says.

"Sweetie, look at me." Genevieve reaches for her daughter's hand.

Parker faces her mother.

"You aren't like anyone; that's exactly right." Genevieve squeezes Parker's thigh.

Parker's an outpatient because her folks fear that centers are places to hook up with bad influences, the Jamie Drakes of the world. When Gary's parents checked him in for alcohol abuse at seventeen, he left with a coke problem. He wasn't going to allow his daughter to go down that road. Parker's grateful; staying in that building would make her miserable.

"So, when do you go back to school, Park?" Finn asks.

"I don't know, Finn." Parker shrugs.

"When will you know?"

"Not sure. Not sure which school I'll be going to."

"You're not sure?" Finn sounds amazed. "I know which school *I* go to."

"I know you do, Finn."

"Blue dropped by again," Genevieve says, switching the subject. "I think he might be waiting at the house."

"Oh." She's too tired for Blue today; too tired to listen to stories about his Goth friends or the midnight Roller Derby league or his boyfriend, Garret, even though she knows he's trying to cheer her up. She's not herself. She can't be happy about ordinary things.

"Mom, I don't want to see Blue right now. Can we just drive around?"

"Sure, honey. We'll just drive."

Parker unrolls her window. The air is crisp. She squints and transforms the meadows into playing fields. She imagines girls in kilts and guys in lacrosse pads chasing a white ball. *Did that place exist?*

When they finally get home, Parker goes for a walk. The Coles live out in the country, and she can walk miles without seeing another house. She meanders through fields, the smell of young grass filling her head. An old well, made of stones, stands defunct but elegant in the meadow.

She sits on its edge. Picks dandelions and pops their heads into the pit.

Where do I go from here?

The mantra in recovery is the Serenity Prayer. *God grant me the serenity to accept the things I cannot change, the courage to change the things I can, and the wisdom to know the difference.* The sky is endless. Parker tries not to think, not to decide, not to give up. A hawk circles.

Just wait. Wait this out. Get to the other side.

Midnight on the beach in the Hamptons. Down a ways from where Noah and Laine are curled into blankets in the dunes, dark bodies sit around a bonfire. The couple hears a bongo beat when the wind carries it this far, but otherwise the night is quiet. Just the surf sliding up the flat sand, tumbling small shells, and then sliding back.

"That was fun today," Noah whispers into her neck.

"I know, I got worn out," Laine whispers back.

Gin-and-tonics are wedged into the sand, bloated lime slices floating. They both stuffed themselves at the clambake, buttering lobster, chowing corn on the cob, wiping their hands on red gingham tablecloths blowing in the wind. They'd felt like royalty, under the American sun, licking their salty fingers and watching kids dance to reggae and splash in the ocean.

"Good times," he whispers.

"The best," she whispers back.

They're kissing. In the dark, Laine eventually feels like there is nothing but Noah.

Stars.

Other guys tried to take Laine apart. When Noah holds her, he's holding her together. Behind them, mansions gleam like sand castles. Reeds shush in night wind.

"I love you," Noah whispers, his hands moving.

"I love you too," she whispers back.

When he pulls down her damp bikini bottom, and kisses her between her legs, he looks up and asks if she's okay. His eyes glow in the moonlight. She nods, unable to speak.

There's an umbrella of sparks in her belly. A flower, blooming with light.

Laine Hunt comes alive.

24

Chase is still in the Hamptons, having stayed at the Lundress guesthouse for a couple of days after the party. He's on his cell phone, sitting in his father's Grand Jeep Cherokee, which Chase still can't believe he loaned him for the Senior Party. Peruvian yard workers are buzzing the privet hedges with loud machines. Chase checks his forehead in the rearview; the bruise is still darkening.

In the end, it was Chase who fared better. O'Mara and MacArthur left two nights ago in Trevor's new BMW X3, their blood staining the graduation present's tan leather seats on the way to the hospital. The PGs did track down Chase and Noah, who were filling up beers at a keg. There had been no chatting this time. Just a haymaker from O'Mara, which grazed Chase's face. But what O'Mara and

MacArthur hadn't counted on was a certain someone waiting patiently nearby for a refill from his best friend. And it didn't take long for Greg Jenson's fists to find O'Mara's jaw and MacArthur's cheekbone.

Randall Dobbs sighs loudly now. "*Why* should I let you go? Do you know how many miles that will put on it?" his dad asks.

"Dad, I understand. I'll make sure the car's in great shape when I come back. I understand this is, you know, a real favor."

"It *is* a real favor," his dad booms. "And how are you going to pay for it? With money you make working on the docks again? That's a summer job that leads nowhere. It's foolish."

"It's good money, and I would pay you back."

"You should work in Carter's office this summer and actually learn something."

Chase swallows. Carter's office. This is a big pawn to hand over so early in the battle, especially when his father sounds like he's still going to say no. His mother is quiet too, even though she's listening to the conversation on the bedroom phone, letting his dad bully him. When his father hangs up, she'll comfort Chase, explaining for the millionth time that Randall is a hard man to please, and he should be patient, *blah blah blah*. Chase's blood simmers.

"I'll gladly work for Carter this summer if you'll let me go," Chase says.

"Well, you should be working there anyway; this isn't about striking a deal," his father says.

And that's it. Chase is about to go berserk.

"Sweetie," his mom says before he can say anything. "Why must you go? Why is this so necessary?"

Chase wishes he could see his mom's face. "I want to bring Moses to Parker. I know it will make her happy. I care a lot about her."

These simple sentences seem to be what Betsy wanted to hear. "I think you should go," she says. "And don't worry about the silly mileage."

Even Randall can't hide his surprise. He hems and haws, but Betsy lays down the law once in a blue moon, and must be obeyed. Chase thanks his father for his permission and then thanks God for his mother.

Chase is bored, calls Noah from the road. Noah just started his internship at a private wealth investment firm in Midtown Manhattan. Chase can hear people in his office, typing, sirens.

"How's it going, man?" Noah says.

"Pretty good. Stopping today at Wellington to grab the dog."

"Awesome. You gotta say hi to Parker for me, give her my best."

"Will do," Chase says, as summer air ruffles his hair.

"And check in with me on the way, okay?" Noah says.

"No doubt. Be good, man."

Chase hears in Noah's voice the thrill and fear of a new world. He's surrounded by suits and money and IQ. And it's okay; the two friends can chase different pots of gold at the ends of different American rainbows. Noah can get a Swiss Alps house one day, can quote stocks on the money market channels, can eat dark chocolate from Brussels until he's not hungry anymore. Chase will pursue God or sobriety, freedom and revolution. He can run off the grid. He will drive to Canada. He'll put his carpe diem to good use instead of just pleasure and self-indulgence.

The highway. He listens to country music, singing with Johnny Cash. Chase fills up at gas stations, buys coffee in a paper cup, and is amazed the acidic liquid doesn't eat right through its container.

Mrs. Jenkins is waiting when he gets to campus, which is a ghost town. She's had Moses groomed, and gives Chase a bag of food, two metal dishes, and a leash. When Chase asks if she's sad to be giving up Moses, she looks away.

"No," she says. "I was sad to give up Parker. Tell her we should have been there for her more often. Tell her I'm sorry."

Chase nods. "I will. I can give you her number, too; I bet she'd love to hear from you."

Mrs. Jenkins gets a pen and paper. Chase scribbles the

number and hands it over. He leaves, letting Moses sniff the tulips and impatiens.

Constantly he thinks about telling Parker he's coming. But the idea of a surprise is too good. Chase does talk to Gary and Genevieve, calling them first from a pay phone at a White Castle in New London, the phone hot in the sun. He calls from Buffalo, New York, too, a day away.

"Yeah, she's coming along," is how Gary answers Chase's inquiry about Parker. His tone is not dishonest, but certainly not telling the whole truth.

"Good, that's good to hear," Chase says, as he's meant to say.

At night, he builds his tent in camping sites he marked on his map. Moses and Chase walk, wherever they are, and then crawl into bed with a Subway sandwich and a Coke. He reads by flashlight, but falls asleep early, by ten, and gets up when dawn arrives rosily through the nylon of the tent.

Chase thinks back to his bullshit notions of free will. Pursuing pursuit. What he realizes now is that he needs to believe in something worth working for, bleeding for, driving across country for, waiting for, someone worth loving, some way that's worth living.

As the car sucks up the dotted line, and the June countryside slides by, he thinks of how beautiful Parker is. Her legs, the way she crosses one over the other, and kicks one foot to the music, playing drums with her thumbs on her thigh. The planes of her face when she's looking dead into his eye. Her stomach, hard and narrow, showing between her T-shirt and black jeans. It's so many hours to drive, he spends some of those hours kissing her, touching her; he thinks about everything he wants. He can't help it.

"How's the open road?" Randall asks when Chase calls from a rest stop over the Canadian border, where a baby's diaper is being changed on a picnic table. His dad sounds like he hopes Chase is doing well.

"So far, so good, Dad," Chase says. "Almost where I need to be."

At night, when Chase clicks off the flashlight, and listens to frogs croak and twigs snap, he has other thoughts. He looks into Parker's chocolate eyes and can't find her. He touches her arm, and it's wet with anxiety. He thinks of how they got to know each other last year in the infirmary. Lying in beds, completely unaware of who the other person really was. They read library books together, and tried to drink chicken broth while the snow fell outside, and joked with Nurse Sinclair, and fought over TV shows. It was so innocent, the sickness they had then. Goddamn egg salad sandwiches gone bad. It was nothing.

"Oh, man," he sometimes says out loud, and Moses turns to him. "It's nothing, Mo," Chase says then. "I was just thinking about your mama."

Chase is so used to talking to the dog that by the time he

arrives in Ottawa, he believes Moses understands.

"You ready to see Park?" he asks, and Moses whines, as if saying yes.

Chase is shaking. He's nervous and excited and he feels like a freak after being in the car so long, arguing with talk radio, singing AC/DC like an opera star, and thinking and thinking and thinking. All he wants is for Parker's face to break from surprise to joy, and for Moses to jump on her. Then he wants to hold her hand while they sit, and he wants her to know he's got her back. He pulls into the driveway.

"Over here!" Genevieve calls from the barn.

Gary and Finn are working on a refrigerator in the shade, and Genevieve is sitting on an overturned bucket. Chase lets Moses out, who runs to them as if he knows them.

"Hey, y'all," Chase says, his many emotions making a mess of his face.

Gary puts down a wrench and gives Chase a bear hug. "Glad you're here," he says.

Genevieve hugs Chase as if he were her son, and Finn holds out a hand for a slap, his eyes full of questions.

"Hey, Finn," Chase says gently, unable to answer him now.

"She's dozing," Gary says. "She wanted to be left alone; she was writing all morning in her journal, but then she wanted to have some space to think, so we let her nod off. Peeked in the window a half hour ago; she's out like a light."

Chase nods.

"Better go wake her up," Genevieve says, and her voice is thick with feeling.

"I will," he says, and he whistles for Moses, who's investigating the dark barn.

The house is heavy with flowering vines and a vegetable garden in back. The cedar-shingled roof has white trim, and wind chimes dangle from the eaves. He steps inside, holding Moses by the collar. He raises a finger to his lips and pantomimes to the dog to be quiet. They tiptoe through the living room, where Navajo blankets cover the couch and aloe plants thrive in pots, the perfume of saffron and basil in the kitchen. The first bedroom is Finn's, with a mobile of the earth and its planets hanging from the ceiling, and a computer on his desk.

The second door in the hall is closed, and Chase taps it. Moses strains. Chase smiles in a spasm of nerves.

"Park," he says quietly.

He opens the door. She's bundled up in her bed, her body curled in a fetal position under a tangerine-orange coverlet. There's a Joy Division poster on her wall. Chase decides Moses should be the one, and he lets go of the collar. Moses bounds up to the bed and snuffs around her legs. Chase watches, grinning.

She doesn't move.

Chase takes a few steps to cross the room, and his legs

272

drag, as if he's wading through syrup. Moses looks at him, as if pleading. Chase tears the sheets off.

There's no one in this bed. The rumple of blankets just happened to look like a silhouette.

He stomps through the house like a wild person, calling her name. "Parker. Parker Cole. Park."

He knows she's not here.

As he walks down to the barn, Gary and Genevieve can tell his stride isn't right and they run to him. As he tells them, they're already slamming around the property, then through the house, calling their daughter, calling and calling.

In the kitchen, Genevieve dials the police, her fingers— bejeweled with silver and turquoise—are shaking. They talk with her, but of course can't do anything yet. Finn holds his cat like something to save from a sinking ship. Gary's on a cell phone, calling Blue and Pete. Chase can tell Gary is working to sound like this is nothing, that it will be fine.

Genevieve paces. She and Gary talk about what she might have done, where she might be. *The library? The video store? Would she really have walked? Would she really have gone without telling us, knowing how upset we'd be?* Chase tries not to get in the way. He picks at his chapped lip.

"Gen," Gary says hoarsely. "I can't find her wallet or phone."

Genevieve looks at him. "But her phone goes right to voice mail."

Chase comes to, as if he'd been in a trance. "Moses," he says, snapping his fingers at the dog. Moses heels, sensing the situation.

Chase walks to the door.

Gary calls his name. "Where are you going?"

"Moses and I are going to look for her. We'll just walk around."

"You don't know where you are," Genevieve says. "You don't know your way."

Chase shrugs, his face drawn. "It's okay."

As he leaves, he feels the bustle start up again in the living room. Moses stays by his side as Chase walks. He heads through a strawberry field, although it's too early for berries. They're upside-down hearts, planted in the earth. Chase is alert, scanning the meadow, the sky, the horizon. Listening for a possibility.

Parker Cole, you'd better fucking wait for me, he thinks, as the dog strains at the leash, gagging, looking for his beautiful master.

Off in one part of the sky, buzzards make circles. Wings tip, and the birds slide. Chase looks like a stranger in a strange land, a guy in Ray-Bans crossing a field under a new sun. Up ahead is a crumbling well, with a vine of morning glories twisted around its bracket. This becomes the lighthouse.

When they're closer, Moses starts whimpering and Chase

loses hold of the leash. The dog runs like he's on fire. Out of the long grass, someone sits up. Parker's in a white sundress, her hair tangled around her face. She shields her eyes with her hand. Now she struggles to her bare feet. The way she got up reminded Chase of playing cowboys and Indians when he was young. You pretended to be dead, sprawled in sweetgrass, and then after a proper time had passed, you were resurrected, alive again, pistol in hand. Ready to play.

"Oh my *God*," is all Parker gets to screech before Moses tackles her to the ground. She laughs while he slobbers on her face, his gigantic paw pinning her down at the sternum.

That dog loves her like crazy.

"Hi," Chase says, walking up to them, hands in pockets and exhaling—smiling, relieved, nervous, happy—a hundred things at once.

Parker finally sits up, hay in her hair, eyes bleary—bleary just from lying in the sun and dreaming. He can tell she's sober. He squats to kiss her.

"Your parents are freaking out," he says.

She rolls her eyes. "We should go back."

He hauls her up, and she brushes grass and ladybugs from her wrinkled dress. Moses rears up and pounces around, like a horse, excited to go anywhere. Above them, the pale blue sky is full of invisible stars.

Parker just keeps looking at Chase sideways and grinning

as they walk. She's at a loss for words. He smells like fast food and car leather, and he's got highways in his eyes. She thought, by some insane logic, that she would never see him again.

Meanwhile Chase is thinking that she looks changed. Marked. More beautiful. Just sitting out there, sunburned nose and shoulders and knees. But the true difference is in her eyes; she knows now that she doesn't know it all. She got schooled. She grew up.

"How did you get here?" she asks as they cross the field.

"I drove," he answers, eyes crinkling at the corners.

"That's not what I meant, really," she says.

He smiles at her, squeezes her hand. "I'm here."

Mainly he's affected right now by the certainty that she still belongs to them. That she may not make it back to Wellington, but she's not cut from the crew. These friends may not share a hometown, but they'll always share some virtual place that exists in the heart or the memory, the past and the future, a space from which no one can expel them. None of them are lost to each other, even strewn across the globe.

Delia's in California, her blond dreads piled on her head as she cuts papaya with a kitchen knife, starting her day. Her summer job is at a juice shop on the beach, where the salty air blows the screen door, making it flap in its threshold through the afternoon.

In a manic and windowless office with AstroTurf for carpet, Noah studies the Wall Street traders he's coveted for so long, and they send him onto the hot New York City sidewalks to pick up deli sandwiches and sodas for their fast lunches. He sweats, crossing alleys, already high on this life.

Greg's sweating, too, on a basketball court in Brooklyn, handing balls to the young day campers whom he's teaching to shoot. His hair's in cornrows, and the big elm towering over the courts provides some green shade but not enough for this day. A guy with an ice-cream cart jingles his bell, and Greg calls a time-out. The kids cheer and line up.

Nikki's on a train, headed to a women's shelter in Queens, where she's volunteering this summer. The *Daily News* is spread in her lap, but she's staring out the dirty window, watching the world of her childhood flicker by, catching a glimpse of two little girls splashing in an aboveground pool in one of the yards.

In a hotel room in Paris, doves hustle on the stone sill. Gabriel is taking a nap before a late dinner with his father and two French government officials. They'll eat oysters and smoke cigarettes and finish with espresso, and Gabriel will be expected to contribute to the conversation like an adult.

Through the haze of pollen and sun, Laine is biting her

lip and driving the family's Wagoneer. Her sister Christine is belted into the passenger seat, watching the new driver navigate the road where their father lives. Laine makes a wide turn into his drive, and he's standing on the slate stoop, waiting, smiling. He's wearing the khaki shorts he wore when they were little, stained with white paint from the tree house he built in the backyard.

And Jamie Drake? He's alone in the dark. He's waking up late in some stranger's house in Westhampton, and making promises to himself. These are promises he's made before. These are promises he's broken. In a dark room like this, he can only make the promises again, and open the door to the light and take his chances.

Chase and Parker get closer to the cedar-shingled house, which sits in a slight valley. They're too far to hear the wind chimes but can see broken mirror bits strung into a mobile that hangs from the eaves. The buzzards are gone from the sky. Someone moves in the lush garden of the house, but no one there has caught sight of the couple yet.

"I can't believe you," Parker says to Chase, putting her arm over his shoulders.

But she can. She can believe him.